THE CHRISTMAS WALK CAPER

A MAC AND MILLIE MYSTERY

JB MICHAELS

HARRISON AND JAMES PUBLISHING

For Becky Jo, thanks for your incredible dedication to your family and steadfast commitment to unending humorous sarcasm.

For Johnny Rogers, thanks for your kindness, dedication to your craft, and enthusiasm for all things sporting.

For the staff of The Little Traveler, thank you all for welcoming me and my work.

THE CHRISTMAS WALK CAPER

CHAPTER ONE

MORNING

Mac O'Malley adjusted his chair in the atrium café of the Tiny Wanderer, a labyrinthine retail center inside a colonial-style mansion nestled on the famously charming Third Street of Geneva, Illinois. He moved his hands closer to the keyboard of his brand new appropriately named Mac computer. He stopped just short of typing when he decided to take a drink of his black coffee that smelled better than it tasted. Alas, that was just the way the former cop and national hero liked it. Bitter, black, and hotter than hell. Many Chicago winters on the beat needed coffee just like this.

As much as Millie would like to point out and Mac deny, he always slurped his coffee. He slurped it now. He realized it when the old gray-haired man lowered a newspaper to reveal a menacing scowl.

"Sorry. Just really love the coffee here." Mac smiled.

The man stared for an uncomfortable pause then put his paper back up to his face.

Mac made a face back at him but only after the older man couldn't see. Time to work. The brand new computer beckoned him to write. Though admittedly, Mac would have rather just watched movies on the amazing screen. He had a hard deadline though. A major New York publisher wanted his story. The true-life story of a cop who prevented an attack on the Chicago marathon through his wits and resolve and apparent willingness to follow a hunch even though it disobeyed direct orders from a superior officer.

Mac hadn't come away from the attack without the weight of severe consequences. He would never be a cop again. Well, a cop in the way he wanted to be. He didn't want the desk job and instead had opted for the big publishing contract and a chance to start anew. The advance was big enough for him to take some time off and figure out his next move.

For now, the chronic pain in his leg would forever be a reminder of his once vigorous job and the fuel that drove him to write the book. He looked to the cane that leaned on the wall next to his small circular table. He sighed, trying not to let it bother him and sink him into a bleak depression. He was told that writing the story would help him and help other cops to inspire them to be the best they could be.

"You got this, Mac. Let's do this." He cracked his knuckles, slurped his coffee again.

The man lowered the paper. Mac winked at him.

Paper back up. Mac wondered how far he could push it with this guy.

He thought better of the possible antagonism and moved his fingers to the keyboard.

"I tried calling her house again and again. She should be here by now," Edith, the hostess in the café, said to another Tiny Wanderer employee, who held garland and a string of lights.

Mac, doing everything he could to not actually write a damn word, looked up from his beautiful, vibrant, blank computer screen. Eavesdropping was a much better idea.

"That is not like Patricia at all. You think someone should go over there? I mean, she lives right behind the store," the employee responded.

"Can you stay here? I will run over there. She

would be here today of all days." Edith walked down a hallway presumably to grab her jacket.

Mac surmised she meant the day of the Christmas Walk. Today was the first day of two where the people of this delightful little burg gathered to light the Christmas tree and then walk through elaborately staged and decorated homes around downtown Geneva, all in celebration of the holidays.

Geneva did Christmas celebrations right. If you couldn't feel the magic of the holidays in this town, then your name must be Ebenezer Scrooge, prehauntings of course. The Tiny Wanderer did great business on this weekend, and Patricia, the owner of the retail mansion, would most definitely be here to greet guests and hand out hot chocolate, etc. You know, Christmassy things.

Mac closed the laptop and put it in his backpack. Put his peacoat on and grabbed his cane. He decided to leave the backpack as it would slow him down. Edith wouldn't mind a former cop joining her for a stroll.

CHAPTER TWO

"Edith, mind if I join you?" Mac hobbled with his cane to the side door of the Tiny Wanderer.

"Officer O'Malley, of course I don't mind. In fact, I am worried about her. Happy you decided to join me. I assume you heard us talking in the café." Edith opened the door for Mac.

"I did. I am sorry. Old cop habits. I have been wondering myself where Patricia was, especially on the most festive weekend of the year. She would have warmed my coffee, and we'd have had our morning small talk by now." Mac walked out on the covered walkway to the wintry December air.

"Luckily, she doesn't live far. How's the leg this morning?" Edith asked as she joined Mac on the walkway.

"Don't worry about me."

The pair walked down the sidewalk and past the back of the Tiny Wanderer to the neighborhood that ran parallel to Third Street. The neighborhood of downtown Geneva was a beautiful, varied, and very expensive place to live. The taxes alone rivalled Mac's gross paycheck in his rookie year. Some houses were traditional Victorian while others were new builds with stonework in the front and beautiful siding and shutters in various colors.

Mac and Edith approached Patricia's ranch home that was hidden behind several trees. Patricia's house only had one floor, but it stretched an entire corner of Fifth Street. There was even greenhouse paneling on one section of the roof that let light in all year round. Patricia had her own version of a year-round garden inside. She loved gardening. Spent hours talking about it.

"That's not a good sign." Mac pointed his cane at an unmarked squad car that he recognized. His brother Vince stood outside of the front door. He waved at the pair.

"Oh dear, no. What happened?" Edith ran across the street to Vince.

Mac shook his head and hurried with his cane, frustrated that Edith was faster than him.

Edith crumpled in Vince's arms.

Mac figured that the reaction meant the worst for Patricia. He walked onto the driveway. His heart pounded in anticipation of the bad news.

"Vincey, what happened? Why are you even here?" Mac asked his brother who still consoled Edith.

"Her house is one of the one's displayed on the Christmas Walk tonight, and Jerry came over to talk with her about the security he would be providing tonight as hundreds of people were to walk through her house to see the decorations. He knocked and knocked and finally just let himself in. That's when he found her," Vince, Mac's taller, silver-haired, handsome brother and Geneva police detective informed.

Edith finally let go of Vince's tan peacoat.

"Who's Jerry?" Mac asked.

"He's a patrolman for GPD. Come on in. I will show you. Edith, do you want to stay out here?"

"I'd better get back to the store and tell everyone, I suppose." Edith wiped her tear-laden cheeks with her sleeve.

A black town car rolled into the driveway next to Vince's squad. The mayor of the delightfully charming town of Geneva emerged from the back seat of the luxury vehicle.

"What the hell happened? Today of all days!" the rather rotund, well-dressed in a suit and tie, and bald politician yelled. He vigorously stomped to Vince, Edith, and Mac's position at the front door.

Vince opened the door. "I am afraid a wonderful citizen of Geneva and owner of the Tiny Wanderer has passed away, Stieg. Looks to be a heart attack from what I can tell, but the medics will be here shortly to sort that out."

"If you'll excuse me. I have to get back to work." Edith made her way back down the driveway.

"Should she be going and blathering about Patricia's demise all about town? This is a big weekend for the Chamber of Commerce. One of the biggest! Let's be real," Stieg, the mayor, said.

Mac felt the urge to stuff his mouth with the business end of his cane.

"These things happen, Stieg. They were close friends. Let her be." Vince urged him to come inside.

"Oh, and your hero cop brother is joining us as well. Uh, Mac is it?"

"Yes, so pleased to meet you, Mayor." Mac rolled his eyes.

As he entered, his stomach tumbled, his heart continued its rapid, rhythmic march, and he took a deep breath to try and calm himself for what he was about to see. The dead body of one of the kinder and more welcoming persons he'd met in his new town.

CHAPTER THREE

Inside Patricia's house, the scent of pine and freshly baked cinnamon buns immediately filled Mac's nose. The entrance of the ranch home gave way to a view of the main living room. Visitors were met just inside the foyer with garland and lights stretched and wrapped around a classic boiler stove. A quick glance to the left and there was a wide Christmas tree decorated with white lights and elegant purple ornaments. Across from the tree was a miniature decorative village that spanned the length of the long bay window. Mac surmised there must have been fifty glass buildings and over a hundred small statues that made up the Christmas village.

It was no doubt a popular and fitting stop on the Christmas Walk.

"She's this way." Vince walked past the living room to the kitchen which was on the other side of the wall the Christmas tree stood next to.

Stieg followed closely. Mac shook his head and followed a few paces behind.

Patricia lay facedown on the wood floor. She wore a nice festive green suit jacket with slacks. A plastic medicine bottle was in her hand, the cap a few inches away from her on the floor and a few pills scattered across the floor. Mac didn't expect to see her in such an unfortunate position.

"Heart pills. She must have suffered a cardiac event and went for her pills but obviously didn't down the pill in time," Vince explained.

Stieg wiped his bald head with a handkerchief from his pants pocket. "So, she had a heart attack and died. It happens. Very common. How long will it take the ambulance to get here? Have you notified her daughter yet?"

"I don't know if she died of a heart attack, Vince. Have you looked around? Done your job yet?" Mac wanted more time at the scene.

"Mac, she was eighty-eight years old. Her heart gave out." Vince shook his head.

Stieg's chest heaved. "Yes, old people die like this all the time. I can't tell you how many wakes I have been to with donors to my campaign who died shoveling snow or whatever else. Heart attacks are common. If Vince, my lead detective, says she died of a heart attack, then I believe it."

"Patricia never mentioned anything about a heart condition to me." Mac walked over to the pill bottle. The label read Levoxythyroxine.

Vince walked to Mac and put a hand on his brother's back. "Mac, she wasn't murdered. She just died of old age. There is nothing more to it. I have to get home. I go on furlough tomorrow, and Tricia is nagging me about helping get ready for our trip. Just stop it. You are retired. Enough. Stop trying to make something out of nothing."

"Oh, so that is why you don't want to work this scene. You are going on vacation. Patricia deserves better." Mac picked the bottle up, pulled himself back up with his cane, and examined the label.

Vince's eyes widened. "Mac, you just moved here three weeks ago for Christ's sake. She probably didn't tell you her health problems because she hardly knows you. Hello! Oh, welcome to Geneva! By the way, I have heart problems. Did I say welcome to Geneva? Why would that even come up in conversation?"

The creak of the door sounded from behind

them. Two paramedics walked into the kitchen with a gurney between them.

Stieg waved the medic over to the dead body. "Get her out of here, please. Also, Mac, could you please leave the premises while we clear Patricia."

"This is a mistake. You should at least pretend like there could be something other than just a heart attack and she's old here, Vince." Mac's eyebrow raised.

"Don't do Dad's eyebrow thing. The mayor is my boss. He wants her out of here. Let this go, Mac. It's Christmas and I haven't even notified her next of kin yet. Drop it. Go write your book already, hero." Vince pushed him out of the kitchen.

Mac didn't resist, but he watched as the medics turned Patricia onto her back. He noticed a bruise on her neck. Small but significant.

"She has a bruise on her neck, Vince." Mac pointed with his cane.

"Mac. Get. Out. I got this. If there is something I think needs to be looked into, I will. Trust me," Vince said.

"Time to go, O'Malley," Stieg urged.

Mac took a deep breath, imagined a rightful caning of the mayor, then turned around. "Let me know if you decide to do your damn job, Vince. Merry Christmas."

Mac had zero plans to stop a private investigation. He would return to the scene of a very possible crime soon.

CHAPTER FOUR

Millie checked her newly dyed hair in the mirror of her place of work, Salem Bank and Trust. Two-toned style with dark roots and silver the rest of the way to her shoulders. Millie's hair legitimately didn't grow longer in a healthy way past her shoulders. Her teeth didn't grow either. She still had baby teeth. At least ten.

Millie had many health problems all remedied in some way by her mother's obsession with natural cures and procedures. Still, Millie, passably, was considered a healthy thirty-year-old woman, tall and very attractive, fair skin, blue eyes, with a calming charm about her. People liked Millie. Mac really liked Millie and Millie really liked him, and life this holiday season was surprisingly good. Very good.

She walked out of the bathroom and back to her desk. Her second morning appointment would be soon. She was a loan officer but also the investment banker and financial planner who handled the particularly large accounts that many held in the affluent 'burb of Geneva. Again, likeable. People wanted to work with her and trusted Millie to do the job right. She had for many years already.

Her desk phone rang. She smiled as she heard his voice.

"Hulloh! Mills. You there?"

"Yes, yes. You didn't even let me respond. You sound hyped? What is it? I have another appointment soon. You know, parents coming in to see if they have enough money to cover their teenage daughter's trip to Vail. Anyway, what's up?"

"Can you do me a quick favor? See what the drug Levoxythyroxine is used for?" Mac's voice burst from the phone's receiver.

"You aren't capable of searching the internet? Why am I doing this, by the way?" Millie asked.

"I don't have a good data connection near downtown for some reason. And I need to know quickly. I thought you would be the best option. Maybe I think too highly of you."

"Ha! Shut it. Levoxythyroxine is thyroid medication. I didn't have to look it up because Grandma uses it. I have had to pick it up for her from the pharmacy a few times," Millie said.

"Thyroid medication. So not heart medication," Mac said.

"Yes, that is what I said."

"Hmm—"

"Mac, what are you up to?"

"I will tell you later. Gotta go. Thanks so much! We have dinner at your mom's tonight, right?"

"Yes, I am warning you she can be very sweet, but she is also super sarcastic. You have to experience it to know how severe it is at times. Then we are going to the lighting ceremony and Christmas Walk too. It will be fun. Your first Geneva Christmas. It will be great."

"Wonderful. See you later!" Mac ended the call.

The rare sound of the dial tone buzzed in Millie's ear. She shook her head. Mac got worked up rather easily. He was an enthusiastic man, and his energy could be infectious. It was part of his charm, but for some reason, she didn't feel great about that last conversation.

A woman with glasses and a poodle walked up to her desk.

Time for her next appointment.

CHAPTER FIVE

Mac waited behind the wide pine tree across the street from Patricia's ranch estate. The ambulance pulled out of the driveway first. Then Stieg's town car. That jerk. Followed by his lazy brother who refused to actually treat the kitchen like a crime scene. Mac hadn't saved thousands of people in downtown Chicago by ignoring his instincts. He hadn't wanted to boast in front of Vince and his boss, but still. Something wasn't right. Patricia showed no signs of poor health. Worked long hours at the Wanderer and ran the place with little stress and ease.

She wouldn't just up and die.

The coast was clear. Mac waited an extra two minutes in case they forgot something inside the house. He walked back to the door. He flipped the bottom of his cane up and unscrewed the rubber stop at the bottom. His lock-pick kit fell out into his palm.

Mac looked at the door handle. There was a bolt lock and a knob lock. He hoped he could get both open in a reasonable amount of time before the daughter made it here or whomever.

Wait.

Where was the original officer Vince had talked about? The one who discovered Pat's body. Jack or Jerry. Jerry? Jerry, that was his name.

Mac looked around at the street. No cars were parked close enough. Jerry was probably gone, too, right?

Whatever. No time to waste.

Mac worked the bolt lock first. The cold air didn't make the use of his fine motor skills easy. The blood rushed away from his fingertips. Mac gritted his teeth and soldiered on. The sound of a car pushing through the winter air on the street caused him to stop then drop one of his picks.

"Shit." Mac looked to the street.

The Cadillac SUV drove past the house.

"Jesus. Mac. Get it together." He bent down, grabbed the pick, and continued his work.

The time off had made him rusty. The surgery,

recovery, and PT did little to sharpen his law enforcement skills. Not that lock-picking was a cop skill but Mac sometimes had very different ideas of what the duties of a cop should be. He was supposed to have been patrolling the marathon route not stepping on the FBI's toes and doing the bomb squad's job. Mac loved being a cop and did whatever it took to get the bad guys. Hence, freezing his ass off trying to break into a new friend's house whom he suspected had been murdered.

The pop sound of the bolt moving into an open position could be heard through the door. Mac tried the handle, and the door opened right up. The security system hadn't been armed. If there even was one. Patricia did say she was reluctant to even put systems like that in the Tiny Wanderer. She was old-school like that.

Mac pulled out his phone. The plan: take as many pictures as possible. See if he could find anything out of the ordinary. Get out quickly. Well, as quickly as possible, given his slower gait.

Mac started snapping as soon as he closed the door behind him. He walked to the kitchen and kept pressing the shutter icon on his touchscreen. Over and over again. The fridge had an elaborate Advent calendar secured to it with magnets that looked like the Tiny Wanderer.

On the calendar, Patricia had a meeting scheduled for today. No other details, just the words 'meeting at noon.' Not very thorough but still good to know. There were other appointments scheduled in November too. Similar in start time. The weekly meeting for the retail workers at the Wanderer? Could be. Mac would be sure to ask around upon his return to the café in a few minutes.

The pills were no longer spread over the wood floor. The rest of the cherry wood cabinets and stainless steel kitchen appliances were spotless. As if nothing had happened. Still, Mac snapped as many pics as possible. He could see no signs of a struggle or even where Patricia kept her pills. Everything was tidy. Mac felt a slight tinge of doubt. Maybe Vince was right. He was trying to make something out of nothing. Too eager to do the police work he so sorely missed at times.

With enough pictures logged into his phone storage, Mac called it quits and walked out of the kitchen and back to the main room. Through the bay window above the vast Christmas village, Mac spotted a minivan pull into the driveway. Probably the daughter. He'd left his old badge in his bag at the

Tiny Wanderer. Not good. He couldn't prove he was a cop or an ex-cop masquerading as an actual cop. He had to hide.

A middle-aged couple emerged from the van and walked to the door. The daughter had short brown hair and looked like Patricia. The presumed husband was very well put together. He looked like he'd just walked out a trendy men's retail store.

Mac had to hide. And fast.

He hobbled over to the Christmas village and ducked under the long card table the village was set on. Patricia had placed a decorative tablecloth on the table that hung low to the carpet. He threw his cane under and rolled under the table.

Hopefully they wouldn't be here long. Mac's leg hurt like hell.

CHAPTER SIX

The daughter sniffled upon entering her mother's house. "I can't believe this. Today of all days. Her favorite weekend. Favorite time of the year."

"Why don't we just come back tomorrow night? We can sort everything out then." A male voice employed a sensitive yet slightly irritated tone.

"Gordon, we have to get the will and see what she wanted as soon as possible for the funeral arrangements, and I just...just want to be here right now. Besides, it will only take a minute. She said she kept it in her top dresser drawer."

Her voice began to fade as she made her way farther into the house.

Mac considered the quick roll out and exit. He started to roll. Mind over handicapped matter. Just do it. Go quick. The daylight's overcast lighting painted the ceiling he looked up at.

The doorbell rang. Twice in rapid succession.

Crap.

Mac rolled back under the table.

"I got it!" Gordon ran to the door.

The door opened.

"Mayor Erikson, how can we help you?"

"I am so sorry for your loss. Is Suzanne here. Can I speak to her?"

"Yes, yes, come on in. Hey, Suzy! The mayor is here!"

Mac rolled his eyes. What an ass. He knew where this was going.

"Coming!" Suzy responded from far away.

"Come on in and sit down." Gordon's voice became louder as he walked into the living room and very close to Mac's location.

Mac didn't know if he should hold his breath. He wanted to bite the handle of his cane. His leg hurt more and more with each passing second.

"I don't want to intrude. I will only be a few minutes. Very busy. Oh, there she is. Suzy, I am so terribly sorry, and you have Mrs. Erikson and I's deepest condolences," Stieg said.

"Thank you. What can we do for you, Mayor?" Suzy asked.

"You see, I am in quite an unprecedented situation. This is one of Geneva's biggest nights of the year, if not the biggest single night of the year. And you and your mother have done such a wonderful job of decorating the house for this year's Walk. I just wanted to ask if we can keep the house open tonight as it is a pillar for our community. We are expecting huge crowds this evening, and even movie and TV studios are sending location scouts for possible filming projects, and I don't want to risk disappointing anyone. I already boasted about your mother's home and business as being the premiere attractions. I understand if you can't grant me this request as everything is very fresh and shocking, but I beg of you, please, keep the house open. The GPD will be here as always to make sure everything goes smoothly," the mayor pleaded.

Mac wanted to puke. He couldn't believe his ears.

"I don't see why not. Right, Suzy?" the husband said. "We have enough on our plate with the kids. The kids don't even know yet. Let's just go ho—"

"Gordon! It is not your decision to make..." Suzy's voice started strong then trembled.

"She would have wanted what the mayor want—"

"Gordon! Stop. Fine. Fine. You can keep the house open for the walk, Mayor. Only because Mom loved her community and wouldn't want the focus to be on her death. Fine. Thank you, Mayor. You can leave now," Suzy said.

Gordon was also a big jerk. Mac took note.

"Thank you so much, Suzanne." The mayor left immediately. The door shut behind him.

"I am sorry, Suzy," Gordon said, but Mac wondered how genuine he was. Why was he so eager to keep the house open for Mayor Meathead?

"I found the will. Let's get back to the funeral home before the kids are done with school." Suzy opened the door.

Their footsteps faded. The door closed again.

Mac rolled out from under the table and let out a big sigh of relief.

CHAPTER SEVEN

Mac made his way out of Patricia's house. He didn't want to have to hide or explain his way out of some ridiculous problem he'd created for himself. He'd snapped a lot of pictures and would sync the pictures to his new Mac he'd left at the atrium café. The big high resolution screen would help him mine the pictures for foul play.

Millie was right. He was hyped, but he also had that hunch he couldn't shake. He walked back to the sidewalk that led to the side entrance of the expansive colonial mansion.

The town car had parked itself right by Mac's favorite entrance. There was no end to the mayor's annoying tendencies. What was he doing? Trying to keep a lid on things? No shame. No respect for the dead at all.

Mac frowned. His intense eyes and furrowed brow looked just like Ebenezer Scrooge as he leaned on his cane rather aggressively and walked swiftly to the doors.

He opened the door and walked into the greeting card department, through lighting, to the bathroom section, and turned right to the atrium café. Sometimes Mac felt walking with his cane made him feel more powerful than the presumptive weakened state one could and probably did assume came with a cane.

Upon reaching the café, he realized he should probably calm down. Patricia wouldn't want him punching the mayor in the face in her beloved Tiny Wanderer.

He found his backpack right where he'd left it. The crabby man must have left, as two dimes were left on the table with his check. Twenty-cent tip. Mac shook his head. What was wrong with people today?

"Edith, Edith. We will make sure she is honored and respected. Trust me. You made the right choice." Stieg Erikson's voiced raked Mac's ears once more as

he watched the portly mayor emerge from the kitchen.

Edith walked out next clearly upset but holding it together. Her mascara was still dry and no longer running down her face like earlier with Vince. She shook her head and watched Stieg walk between a row of tables toward Mac.

Mac took his seat. The mayor approached. The moment neared. Mac smirked with adolescent glee as he opened the lid to his Mac laptop.

Stieg wiped his bald head and kept a steady pace.

Three feet away.

Mac slipped out his cane ever so slightly into the walking lane.

So close.

"AH!" The mayor of Geneva tumbled to the ground with a loud smack.

"Oh dear, you okay?!" Edith ran over.

"I am fine. I am fine. The Wanderer will have a lawsuit on their hands if you don't create bigger walking lanes in here." The mayor pulled himself up rather quickly much to Mac's minor disappointment.

The tumble was so worth it. Mac had his back to the fall. He ignored Stieg and smiled into his beautiful computer screen.

"I have much to do." Stieg exited the café.

"Officer O'Malley, I saw what you did." Edith sat down across from him.

"What do you mean?" Mac's bottom lip jutted. He held his arms out to his side, palms up.

"I saw what you did, and thank you." Edith laughed, a much-needed catharsis for a terrible start to the day.

Mac joined in. "He fell pretty hard too!"

They laughed hysterically.

Edith rubbed her right temple then took a deep breath. "Pat always thought he was a buffoon."

"He is an ass. Speaking of Patricia, Edith, I noticed on her calendar she had a meeting scheduled for noon today. What was that for?"

"I run all the meetings here so she wouldn't have written that down. Those meetings are always in the morning. She must have had a meeting with Lacy's again."

"Lacy's? You mean the retail giant? Thanksgiving Day Parade Lacy's?" Mac grabbed a pen and his moleskin notebook he'd used to plan his memoir.

"Yes. *The* Lacy's. She wanted it hush hush. She was considering selling the Wanderer to them," Edith said.

"Wonderful. Wonderful! Something to go on.

Anyone else know about Patricia's intent to sell?" Mac scribbled into his notebook.

"Just her daughter, and I assume her son-in-law. Why do you ask? Did you see something Vince didn't see?" Edith's eyes widened.

"I just want to check things out. Make sure no foul play was involved. I owe it to Patricia. She was the first person to welcome me here—"

"You think she may have been murdered?" Edith leaned over with a whisper.

"Don't be alarmed. I just have a hunch. I am just doing my job...well, former job, but still. Do you know where she was to meet with Lacy's people?" Mac shifted in his seat, his leg aching.

"I think they usually met at the Hennington Inn next to the Fox River. They met in the restaurant lounge there once before. The rep came from New York and stays there, of course."

"Edith. Thank you for your help."

CHAPTER EIGHT

Millie rubbed the back of her neck. Sitting at a desk, not fun. A far cry from her days as a college athlete. Her cell phone buzzed in the desk drawer. She pulled it open. The typical 'call me when u get a chance' message displayed on her home screen from none other than her mother, Becca.

Millie sighed. The last appointment took too long, and she just didn't want to talk to anyone right now. Still, she picked up the phone and called Mom.

"Hello. I'm at the store. Do you think Mac likes vegetables? Yes. No. Maybe I shouldn't get them. I mean, maybe just baked beans?" Becca said.

"Mom. Slow down. Mac isn't into vegetables. Don't even worry about it."

"I will just get everything. Just make everything.

I mean, it can't hurt. One thing our family likes to do is eat." Becca continued to talk without any acknowledgement that her daughter had responded.

Millie rubbed the side of her face. Why was everyone so hyped today?

"Mom! Why did you call?"

"Well, sorry. Just wanted to make sure we had what Mac likes."

"Whatever you make, I am sure will be fine."

"I'll just get all of this. That's fine."

"All of what? Mom, I have to go. Have an appointment."

"Oh, okay. Talk to you later. Byeeee."

"See you later." Millie ended the call, confused as to what had just happened.

Her phone buzzed again. Mac.

"Hello."

"Hello." Mac's welcome voice comforted.

"Hey. How are you?" Millie asked.

"I'm good. Great actually. You ready for this? I think Patricia may have been murdered."

"Wait, what? Who is Patricia?" Millie looked around and decided to stand up, get out of the bank lobby, and up the stairs to an empty office space.

"Patricia Flaherty, the owner of the Tiny Wanderer. She was found dead in her kitchen this morning. My brother thinks it may have been a heart attack, but she was found on the floor and was trying to take her thyroid pills, not blood pressure pills. Vince said a patrolman named Jerry assigned to do security for her house on the Christmas Walk tonight found her. I don't know, something just doesn't feel right. She was usually in such good spirits and never once talked about a heart condition."

"Oh no. That is terrible, Mac. She seemed like such a nice lady. Maybe your brother is right. We bank with—or banked with—her. She was in her eighties, right? I mean, these things happen. The thyroid pills instead of heart medication doesn't mean she was murdered." Millie paced the empty office space.

"I know. I know. But she was worth a lot of money, and Edith said she was in talks with Lacy's to sell the Tiny Wanderer. When big money is involved, you just never know. I want to do my due diligence and do what my brother is not doing which is investigate. Which is why I am calling you…" Mac said.

"I mean, I really don't think this is necessary. What do you want me to do?"

"You said Patricia Flaherty and the Tiny

Wanderer have accounts with Salem Bank?" Mac asked.

"I was hoping you wouldn't ask that. But yes. Yes, she does. And yes, a personal account and business. One of our bigger accounts. Not the biggest. But big enough. You want me to see if anything strange has been going on in her accounts." Millie sighed and shook her head, worried that Mac's behavior was indicative of his injury and retirement from the force.

"I mean, it can't hurt to look. Maybe some insight as to why she was looking into selling. Thank you, Mills!" Mac's voice abruptly stopped. He'd ended the call.

Millie walked back down the stairs, audibly blowing air from her mouth in apparent exhaustion of having to talk to two of the most hyper people she knew in a very short amount of time.

CHAPTER NINE

Mac stared at the mesmerizing screen of his laptop at all the pictures he'd taken of Patricia's kitchen and house. Nothing seemed to stand out. He looked closely at all the pics of the kitchen. The cherry cabinets, new appliances. Everything was spick-and-span. Super clean. No breakfast mess. Nothing. Did Patricia even cook?

He didn't notice any glasses on or around the sink. If Patricia was going to take a pill, where was her glass of water? Unless of course she'd suffered the cardiac event before she could even procure a glass. Mac wondered where she kept her pills. In a kitchen cabinet? Upstairs in the bathroom? Her bedroom? He needed to get back into the house.

Trusty lock picks to the rescue again. Too many things to check out.

Yet again, he couldn't risk being caught in the house, although now he had his badge. He grabbed his backpack and unzipped the front pocket, and there it was. Yes, it said "retired" at the bottom, but he could cover it with his hand if he needed to flash the badge.

Wouldn't be the worst idea to head back there and hope that the daughter came back. He could ask her a few questions. He had time before the noon meeting at the Hennington. Mac looked at his watch. Eleven ten a.m.

Mac sometimes struggled with focus. If there was much to do or if he thought he had much to do, sometimes his propensity to juggle too many thoughts, plans, ideas in his head caused him some mental lapses in logic. Now he realized he should have stayed in the house after the daughter and husband left, but for fear of getting caught or being forced to hide again, he'd exited the house. Of course, his scatterbrained ways did eventually lead him to a place of careful and deliberate moves. Moves that saved lives.

Everyone has their own methods. If the methodology led to positive outcomes, then so be it.

He grasped his cane and almost lifted from the chair when he decided to stick to his initial plan and continue to examine the pictures he'd taken once more, and more thoroughly this time. Again, his plan to examine the pictures faced considerable opposition to the chaos of his excited mind. He almost stopped that task to return to the house.

He clicked through the many pictures of Patricia's kitchen, put a fist under his chin, and leaned into the screen. He squinted. A reflection. In the glass of the microwave door. He pushed the magnifying glass icon and zoomed in.

The microwave was raised above the stove framed by the cherry wood cabinets above and to the sides of it.

He cocked his head.

He could see a faint image of himself snapping the pic from an angled position on the other side of the kitchen. And...

It appeared that he wasn't the only person in the house. Someone stood behind him in the doorway to the kitchen?! Admittedly, the image was very pixelated and blurry at the current magnification.

Mac rubbed his eyes and tried to discern if someone loomed behind him. His uncertainty bothered him. He immediately cropped the reflective microwave door and sent it to Millie for another pair of eyes.

CHAPTER TEN

Millie's phone buzzed again. A text message. A pixelated image of Mac's reflection in a microwave door. She shook her head. No, she didn't see anyone else in the reflection. She called her eager sleuth of a boyfriend.

"Mac. I don't see anyone in the reflection. I think you should just calm down."

"Really? Not even in the upper right-hand corner behind me? Look behind me," Mac insisted.

"No. No. Stop. Listen, I checked out Patricia's accounts. There has been some recent activity that wouldn't necessarily be flagged by the bank but still substantial enough to mention." Millie typed more on her keyboard.

"Are you sure? There may be someone behind me in the upper right—"

"Mac, did you hear what I just said?"

"I...did."

Millie rolled her eyes. She ignored his ignorance and continued. "Patricia withdrew a considerable amount of cash in the last month or so. About forty thousand dollars. All cash. No wire transfers or cashier's checks. All cash. Why?"

"That is interesting. If she was planning on selling and thus, making money. Why withdraw? Maybe she was also planning a move out of Geneva or out of her house too? A down payment perhaps?"

"That could be it. You should really talk to the daughter. Or maybe you have already? And see if she knows anything about the money. A lot of times people take that kind of cash out, family could be involved. Maybe she was using the money to help them out," Millie said.

"Funny you should mention that. Her and her husband were at the house earlier. Both of them should have been at work, right?" Mac said.

"Yes, but when you get a call that your mother died, you don't have to be at work anymore. Most bosses are understanding."

"True. I will have to talk to her at some point.

Hey, can you meet me for lunch at the Hennington? I want you to come with me and ask the Lacy's rep a few questions. Sound good?"

Millie perked up, excited to get out of the bank and do some investigative work. "I can do that. I will meet you out front. What are we going to ask them?"

"Just about the transaction, the negotiations, Patricia. Anything that can help us figure out what may have happened to her. With a big withdrawal, a sudden death, possible huge life change selling the stalwart retail palace of downtown Geneva to a big company, we could find motive for a murder in that, Mills. We could be onto something here."

CHAPTER ELEVEN

AFTERNOON

Mac decided he would walk to the Hennington. Walking helped him clear his mind and focus his thoughts, and well, engage in the act of actual thinking. Away from the distractions of his computer and having to actually sit down and write the memoir that was due to his editor in New York soon.

With his customary for December Santa hat on, Mac walked with a certain pep in his step, and the cane almost seemed unnecessary. He was a man on a mission and not a mission to go and write about past heroics. Along Third Street, there were holiday decorations everywhere. Lights on the banisters of the subsequent storefronts. Garland wrapped around the light posts. Wreaths on every entrance.

The courthouse tree stood tall at twenty-five feet, fresh, full, and ready for the lighting ceremony this evening.

Mac swore he saw various branches moving inexplicably at different spots in the tree. Were there chipmunks inside it? He stopped his brisk walk for a second to examine the tree. As soon as he stopped, the branches stopped moving. He then saw an ornament fall from the tree and then suddenly zip back into position. He rubbed his eyes with his leather-gloved hands. He squinted again, shook his head, and continued his walk.

"What the heck was that?" Mac said.

The second time in a matter of minutes, his eyes played tricks on him? First the microwave picture and now an enchanted tree. Mac hoped he wasn't losing it.

No snow. Just freezing temperatures at a not too bad twenty-nine degrees with no wind. Thankfully. His Santa hat did much to keep his head warm. The Hennington was about seven minutes away but felt farther in the cold. He'd made it to the main thoroughfare, Rt. 38, and took a right and headed downhill to the inn, which was parallel to the Fox River.

In the distance, on the sidewalk in front of the inn, she stood. Tall. Blonde. Beautiful. The love of his life. Millie. She waved at him and smiled. His heart warmed. He hadn't actually told her how he actually felt. It hadn't been that long, but he knew in his heart. He knew he'd found his person.

He made his way down to Millie and gave her a big hug.

"Glad you could make it! Let's head in there." Mac let go and put his arm out to indicate she go first.

"Why, thank you, sir. Do we know who these Lacy's people are? What they look like?" Millie walked ahead to the door of the pale limestone and wooden construction of the three-story Hennington Inn.

"We will figure it out. Probably people dressed in suits, one would think. Maybe only one or two. I will flash my badge and ask them a few questions." Mac opened the door for Millie.

The lobby of the Hennington was quaint yet posh, with a grand, curved staircase adorned with lit garland. A Christmas tree stood next to the fireplace on the left side of the room across from the staircase. The light tan tones of the lobby were accentuated by the soft lighting and cozy feel.

"Welcome to the Hennington," a young woman behind the check-in desk greeted them.

Mac looked to his right before reaching the staircase. "We're here for lunch. Thanks. Merry Christmas."

"Oh wonderful. Merry Christmas to you as well."

Mac and Millie made their way behind the staircase to the small bar that served as the entry point to the ByWater Restaurant, and where Mac assumed the meeting place for the Lacy's representative and Patricia was.

There were only two men in the restaurant who sat at a table near a window that looked out to the Fox River. Mac noted the ByWater's elegance with high-backed Victorian chairs, limestone walls, and the exposed wood beams shooting across the canopied ceiling. A proper place for wheeling and dealing clients.

"That must be them. Why are there two?" Mac asked.

"My guess is one of them is probably a lawyer. Makes me think Patricia was looking to seal the deal today. Take the hat off," Millie suggested.

"Right. You go over there first. You're the prettier one." Mac nodded his head toward the two men as he took his Santa hat off.

"No, absolutely not. Nope."

"Fine, we go together."

Mac and Millie walked to the table. Both men were dressed in business suits. One bald and older, the other younger and bearded.

"Gentlemen, are you waiting for Ms. Patricia Flaherty?" Mac flashed his badge but kept his index finger over the 'retired' moniker.

"Ah, yes. Yes. You look familiar." The bald one put down his glass of water.

"Would you mind if we ask you a few questions? Nothing to be alarmed about. I understand that Patricia was looking to sell her business to Lacy's," Mac pushed, hoping to skirt the bald man recognizing him from the marathon incident.

The bald one looked at Millie then the bearded man as if to see if it was okay to answer.

The bearded one nodded his approval.

"Terence Mackey. I am with Lacy's Department Store. Please have a seat." Terrence, the bald one, gestured to the seat across from him.

Mac wondered had Millie not been with him, would he have been so cooperative?

"Thank you, gentlemen." Mac pulled out the chair closest to the window for Millie then sat down across from Terence.

Millie took over. "Terence, this may shock you,

but Patricia passed away this morning. How long did you know Patricia?"

"Dear Lord, that is awful. She was so kind. A class-act." Terence's brow furrowed. Eyes glistened with tears.

"We understand. Patricia was wonderful. This is a shock to the community," Mac said.

"We have been negotiating for the past two months. We started in October. Today was the day we were going to finalize the transaction. This is David, and he's the lawyer with the paperwork ready for her to sign." Terence pointed to bearded David.

David just jotted down notes in silence. Mac wanted to throw his pen across the room.

"Did you notice any unusual behavior in Patricia? Or maybe even issues with her health?" Mac asked.

"No. Not at all. She was as fit as a fiddle, energetic, and one helluva good businesswoman. The deal we made certainly skewed to her benefit more than Lacy's. We just really value the property here in Geneva."

"How exactly did she leverage such a good deal from you?" Millie said.

Again, Terence looked at David. David nodded and jotted.

"Well, she did have an offer from another interested party." Terence leaned back in his chair and folded his arms across his chest.

"She used that offer to drive up the price, and Lacy's has a much bigger wad of cash to throw around," Mac said.

"Yes, that is one way to put it."

"Do you know the other interested party?"

"Fanucci."

"Fanucci of Fanucci's Restaurant on Third Street?" Millie asked.

"How did you find the identity of the other buyer?" Mac asked.

"Patricia told me," Terence said.

Mac knew there was no way of proving that statement with Patricia dead. Terence probably sent David to investigate the identity of the other buyer. Whatever. He and Millie now had more to do. Still, it bothered him.

"She just offered that information up?" Mac pushed.

Terence looked upset. "I like to think we became more than acquaintances and businesspeople. Patricia was a friend."

Millie stood up from her chair. "Thank you for your time, gentlemen. I am sorry your transaction didn't go through. Please give the family some time before you contact them."

"We will. We will." Terence sighed and rubbed his bald head.

Mac and Millie walked out of the ByWater and the Hennington.

CHAPTER TWELVE

Millie patted her stomach. "I am starving. Luckily, I packed a lunch this morning."

"After all that, you can just think of food?" Mac laughed.

"I don't think you understand. We Padersons love to eat. I need to eat." Millie walked back to her small sedan in the lot in front of the lobby entrance.

"Mills, we have so much more to do. Fanucci. We must go question Fanucci. Don't leave me."

"I need to get back to work, Mac. Do you want a ride back home or to the Wanderer?." Millie opened her car door.

"Yes, thank you. To the Tiny Wanderer, please." Mac opened the passenger door and climbed inside.

The old car started after a slight delay. She

needed a new one. Mac thought that might be a great Christmas present but probably too much.

"There are a few things at play here, Mac. The Geneva Chamber of Commerce is not especially friendly to big corporations wanting space on Third Street. That is what Randall Road is for. The charm and elegance of Third Street is sort of protected from outside intrusion. There isn't even a Starbrick's on Third south of 38." Millie turned on the radio to a station that played all Christmas music. An instrumental version of "Good King Wenceslas" played.

"So, the Chamber of Commerce would not have been exactly thrilled at the prospect of having Lacy's owning an iconic piece of real estate on Third Street for fear of a big-business approach to a predominantly charming small business, old-town feel of that shopping and dining corridor. The corridor that Ellen deemed one of the most charming towns in America. Got it. We have to question the Fanucci family."

"My question is would the Chamber of Commerce or Fanucci actually murder Patricia to preserve Third Street? Seems rather extreme. Patricia is within her legal rights to sell to whomever she wants." Millie turned onto Third Street.

"Exactly. She did. This may go high into the

power players of Geneva, or maybe the Fanucci family was angry that Patricia rejected their offer and offed her. Why does that name sound familiar?"

"Fanucci?" Millie stopped the car in front of the Tiny Wanderer.

"Yes, wait a minute! They were bootleggers during Prohibition and worked with Capone!"

"How do you know that?"

"The other day I walked into the history museum. There was one picture of a few guys sitting on barrels of beer in the 1920s. The caption of one of the guys in the pic's name was Fanucci! The mob!"

Millie shook her head. "Mac. You have a very active imagination. Please get out of the car. I am starving. I need to get back to my lunch."

"Okay. Okay. Sorry. I am out. See you later." Mac kissed Millie and left the car to the sidewalk in front of the Tiny Wanderer.

"Be nice to the Fanuccis. I played softball with their daughter." Millie leaned over and shot Mac a look.

"I am always nice!" Mac waved as she drove away.

CHAPTER THIRTEEN

Fanucci's opened at three p.m., if the sign across the street was to be trusted.

Mac's stomach growled. Lunchtime. He walked back into the Tiny Wanderer. The store grew busier as the day wore on. More and more people filled the department rooms of the colonial house. He patiently wove his way through the crowd. He went back to the atrium café and ordered a sandwich from Edith.

"How is it going? Any news?" Edith brought him his grilled cheese sandwich and fries.

"Yes, actually. Take a seat." Mac took a big bite of his sandwich and wiped his mouth with a napkin.

"Patricia was going to close the deal today with

Lacy's. Lacy's would have become sole owner of the Tiny Wanderer."

"Oh my." Edith put her hand to her mouth.

"Yes, which makes my murder theory that much stronger. Lots of money involved. Did you know about another buyer?" Mac grabbed a fry.

"No. Patricia only mentioned Lacy's to me. Who is it? Who is the other buyer?"

"According to Terence, the Lacy's liaison, the Fanucci family, owners of the finest dining establishment across the street." Mac took a drink of water.

"Why would Michael want the Wanderer?" Edith asked.

"That is what I intend to find out at three when they open. How are you doing? How is the rest of the team doing?"

"We are upset but keeping it together for work. Keep doing what you are doing, Officer O'Malley. We are all very concerned." Edith stood up.

"I will do the best I can." Mac nodded. He realized that he'd probably put undue stress on Edith. A tinge of regret, possibly doubt, compromised his confidence for a few seconds. He was torn. He didn't want Patricia to be a murder victim, but the hunch he felt was just too strong to ignore.

He opened his laptop. Opened up the notes application and typed. He reviewed the day thus far.

The thyroid pills. Patricia facedown on the floor. She was dressed. Ready for work, ready to face the day. The bruise on her neck...

The bruise on her neck. A small bruise but what could have caused that?

A needle. A needle could have caused it.

Mac searched the internet for bruises caused by needles. A bruise could form if no pressure was applied after the needle was removed. The murder weapon: a poisonous needle?

She was then laid on the floor or fell on the floor. He didn't know and couldn't remember if she had a bump on her head or how she could have fallen. He needed more time to examine the body. Damn mayor, and shame on his brother. He needed to know if there were any physical signs of a fall.

He grabbed for his phone and dialed his brother Vince.

"Yes, Macadamia Nut, what's going on?" His gregarious brother's voice burst into his ear.

"Where is Patricia? I need to examine her body." Mac's tone. Not friendly.

"Already done. Listen, I had the examiner look at her with me. I did do my job after the mayor left. I also took a blood sample and sent it out to the lab. Full toxicology report will be back in a few weeks. This is not the movies or a TV procedural. These things take time."

"Did you check for any signs of falling? Any additional bumps or bruises?"

"No."

"No, there were no bumps and bruises or no, you didn't check?" Mac persisted.

"No, meaning there were no signs of bumps and bruises from falling."

"She fell to the kitchen floor with zero bumps or bruises?"

"Correct. That is possible, Mac. She was fully clothed and not a big and tall woman. She didn't have far to fall," Vince said.

"I trust you found the bruise on her neck that I pointed out earlier."

"That is what bothered me and prompted me to order the toxicology report. It looks like bruising from a needle puncture. All this is being handed off to another detective. Remember, I am going on furlough in like three hours. Mac, we will handle everything from here. Just enjoy the holidays, man. Gotta go." Vince ended the call before Mac could tell him his leads.

CHAPTER FOURTEEN

Millie's anxiety seemed under control, but it wasn't time for her to leave yet. She knew in about an hour and a half the worry would naturally get more intense. Her boyfriend would be heading to 272 WitchHazel Circle for dinner with her family for the first time. She didn't think she would be aiding Mac in a murder investigation either. She hadn't seen such a voracious and intense side of the usually happy-go-lucky Mac she'd come to know.

Nothing new for Millie. Her mother's intensity was ever present, and no stopgap existed. Her father gave up trying to calm her down years ago and just rode the wave. Mac was not at all like her mother in many ways, but today, their energy did match up.

Millie milled about the bank lobby, fiddling

with the holiday decorations. The fake Christmas tree needed a little something, and she would never let Fred decorate the lobby ever again. The ornaments were all scrunched near the top of the tree. They were interest rate ornaments, but still, spread the love, Fred. Idiot. She promptly balanced the ornaments on the tree to have a more even distribution.

No more appointments today and she'd finished the paperwork from prior meetings already. Her efficiency led her to boredom at times. She sat down at her desk, picked up a pen to tap the desk, then decided to check the Fanuccis' accounts for fun. Kill the time.

The restaurant business showed little growth with a steady, rhythmic sum over and over again. Italian food must be very cheap to make. The Fanuccis had lots of money. They certainly held the correct amount of assets to buy the Tiny Wanderer. Millie valued the retail legend at approximately ten million or so, including the real estate.

Nothing out of the ordinary. Perhaps the younger family members wanted to grow their assets and expand into retail.

She would be interested to see what Mac found out.

Speak of the devil. Mac's name lit up on her phone screen.

"Hello, what's the news?"

"Lots of news actually. Firstly, I am excited to head to your parents. It will be great to meet them! Also, Vince actually did help, and he thinks she may have been murdered with a poison syringe. Alas, toxicology reports take forever. I noticed a bruise on her neck, and she had no bumps or bruises on her body, which means someone punctured her neck with the needle, then gently laid her down on the kitchen floor."

"Whoa, so definitely a homicide." Millie spoke softly so no one else could hear, especially Fred in the cubicle next to her.

"Yes, that's what we think. Also Edith, a close friend of Pat's at the Wanderer, said that Patricia never told her about the Fanucci offer. Why not?" Mac asked.

"That is odd. She didn't want Edith knowing about that. We have got to talk to the daughter soon. She will probably know the most about this. Make it to see Fanucci yet?"

"Heading there now. Meet you at 272 at four."

"Get ready. That's when the real craziness begins." Millie laughed.

"I look forward to it. Okay, bye."

"See you soon." Millie wanted to say 'love you' at the end of the conversation. He hadn't said it yet. She felt it. She was fairly certain he felt the same, but he had yet to say it.

Push the lingering miniscule doubt away. He is crazy about you.

CHAPTER FIFTEEN

Mac loved grilled cheese sandwiches but also admitted he felt quite full after the indulgence. Mac had eaten two kinds of sandwiches his whole life— PB and Js and grilled cheese. He hoped he had enough room for dinner. Well, he must have enough room for dinner. He would find a way to eat as much as he could within reason. Didn't want to be rude to Becca and Hank.

Speaking of food, Mac secured his backpack to his back, gripped his cane, and made his way out of the Tiny Wanderer, which had been increasingly more crowded. The ceremony and houses for the Christmas Walk would be open soon. Edith and the team prepared free hot chocolate for shoppers. Bing Crosby's voice resounded through the Tiny

Wanderer, adding an extra special touch to the meticulously decorated rooms of the special retail destination.

Christmas lights of varying color, intensity, even various themes of decoration in the different rooms of the colonial retail mansion added to the celebration of the season. The bathroom/toiletries room was decorated in pink and white. The lighting and lamp room was in blue and gold with various blinking lights, some flashing, others slowly glowing.

Mac made his way to the toy room which had the traditional green and red motif. He wanted to buy a toy to donate. He scanned the room and found a display carousel with various puppets hanging from it. He grabbed one that looked like a bear and another that looked like a frog and would request to have them wrapped together.

For a minute, Mac got swept up in the season. He realized that Patricia would be proud of her team at the Wanderer. The place looked great. Magic filled the air. They'd soldiered on without her and were doing a great job.

His resolve to figure out who stabbed Patricia in the neck with a needle and killed her strengthened.

Mac placed the puppets on the counter and grabbed for his wallet in his jacket pocket.

A young woman behind the counter asked, "Will this be all? Would you like them gift wrapped?"

"Yes, please, both in the same package if at all possible," Mac said.

He realized that only sometimes people recognized his face from his heroic exploits. Others were oblivious, and he liked that. His life had changed enough. Young people who didn't pay much attention to the news definitely didn't recognize him. Mac paid for the toys with his debit card.

She wrapped the puppets quickly and efficiently as a line formed behind him.

"Thank you." Mac smiled.

"Merry Christmas," the young woman said.

"And to you." Mac grabbed the bag and made his way to the exit.

Time to see Michael Fanucci.

Dusk had fallen over Third Street. The temps dropped a little more. Probably twenty-five degrees Fahrenheit.

The Christmas lights started to intensify in brightness as the sun set.

Cars lined the street. People milled about and filled the sidewalks. The Christmas Walk had begun.

Mac crossed the street to the cast-iron work

entrance of the elegant Italian restaurant known as Fanucci's.

He walked in and smelled a hint of garlic, olive oil, and wine. The blend was comforting to Mac. His family frequented an Italian restaurant when he was young. There were gold lights everywhere and green garland along the ceiling of the main dining room which was all glass panes that gave full view of the magic of Third Street during Christmastime.

A young, bushy-eyebrowed man in a suit greeted him. "Hello, sir, do you have a reservation?"

"I don't actually. I was wondering, is Michael in?"

"Michael is not here at the moment. He will be in later. May I take a message?"

"No, no, that's all right. I will come back to see him later. Thanks."

Mac thought it best not to push it any further. He walked out of the restaurant and would head to 272 WitchHazel Circle.

No sooner had he let go of the door than he saw the town car. The mayor's town car. Soon the bumbling baldy would emerge from the black vehicle. Mac stared at the door.

No bumbling idiot yet.

Mac continued down the walkway that led away

from the restaurant entrance and turned right to get back to his vehicle. He felt a hand on his back.

"The mayor wishes you a merry Christmas, Officer O'Malley. He wanted to personally thank you for taking up residence here in Geneva," a deep voice bellowed. A big mitt patted his back. Hard.

Mac turned around, and a large man in a tan, full-length coat walked in the opposite direction and entered the driver's seat of the town car.

Mac gripped his cane in anger. He wanted to knock the guy for a loop. Well, the mayor had just cemented himself as a suspect. With what Millie had said about the Chamber of Commerce maintaining tradition along this charming street, the mayor's meddling may go farther than maintaining his precious Christmas Walk event.

CHAPTER SIXTEEN

At 272 WitchHazel Circle, Millie drove into the subdivision to her parents' house. She neared the green gate that always seemed rather superfluous to Millie. No other home had a gate that led into the driveway except 272. She hit the gate opener in her car and drove down the blacktop driveway. Her parents' house was a brightly colored two floor, four bedroom colonial-style home combined with medieval architecture. Spires shot out from the roof at the edges, and the center entrance looked like a gothic tower as if signifying a church bell. There was no bell.

If the house ever fell into disrepair, it would certainly gain a reputation as being the most haunted house in Kane County. Millie imagined the bright yellow of the painted siding fading into a dull grey. The bushes under the windows growing untouched and wild with ivy crawling up the siding fit for a perennial haunted house attraction.

She hoped her mother would behave. The house was already overwhelming.

Millie walked into the house with her own key. The entrance was grand with a high ceiling, a large chandelier, and a staircase with banisters accentuated with lit garland.

"Hellooooo!" Becca called from the kitchen.

"Hey, Mom. Need any help?" Millie made her way to the kitchen through the hall to the right of the staircase.

"Food-wise, we are good. Could you set the table?" Becca chopped celery on the kitchen counter. She looked a lot like Millie except older.

"Yes, I can do that." Millie walked to the cabinets that lined the bottom of the island in the center of the kitchen.

"Mil, does he know?" Becca asked.

"Mom. No. He doesn't know. We have had this conversation many times. He does not know." Millie placed the plates on the table.

A loud snore resounded from the living room.

"Hank! Wake up! Millie's here and her

boyfriend is coming in a few minutes! I swear I am going to kill your father," Becca yelled at her husband.

"Mom he wakes up at 4:30 in the morning for work. Give him a break. Hey Dad?"

"Oh, hey, Millie!" Hank didn't move from his seat on the couch. He just stared at the hockey game on television.

Millie could see the white hair that sprouted from the top of the couch and smiled. Some things never changed.

The gate bell rang.

"Here he comes. Hank, get up," Becca said.

"I got the gate." Millie put the last plate on the table, walked to the door, and buzzed Mac in.

Mac's powder blue sedan made its way up the driveway.

Becca strode up to Millie in the foyer. "Millie, I think you should tell him sooner than later. Just saying. I think it's important that he knows. Also, your father and I are very happy for you. We haven't seen you this happy in a long time."

"Mom, I know. I know and thank you." Millie opened the door. She reeled from her mother's intensity followed by a really sweet comment and took a deep breath.

Mac walked up the walkway.

"Hey, come on in!"

"Hello! What a day!" Mac stepped into the house.

"What does he mean? What happened today, Millie? What are you not telling me?" Becca asked.

"Mom...I know it has been a weird day. Glad you made it. Mac, meet Becca, my mom."

Becca put out her hand. "Pleased to meet you. I have heard nothing but awful things."

Mac laughed. "Nice to finally meet you too!"

Becca had cut any and all first-meeting tension out of the moment with her humor.

"Lovely home you have here. Love the Christmas decorations." Mac gestured to the garland.

"Thank you. I know I have much more to put up. Oh my gosh. It's ridiculous. Anyway, thank you. So why exactly are you dating my daughter? She's a disaster," Becca continued sarcastically.

Mac and Millie both laughed. A good start.

CHAPTER SEVENTEEN

EVENING

Dinner went smoothly. Well, as smoothly as possible. Millie thought Mac might have been overwhelmed by all the food packed onto the table and the blistering pace with which conversation took place at the dinner table, but he took it in stride. Millie felt good about the situation. It was nearing six p.m. and almost time to get a spot for the tree lighting ceremony downtown in front of the courthouse.

"I am telling you that a fox disappeared in the field. Just gone," Hank said to Mac.

"What happened to it?" Mac asked.

"Bigfoot. No other explanation."

"What do you mean?"

"We walked over after a few minutes and saw nothing but deep marks in the ground." Hank's eyes were wide.

"Wow. That is very strange."

"Dad, we'd better get going. Mac and I are going to head to the Christmas Walk," Millie said.

"Before you go. What is happening? Why was the day so crazy?" Becca put her finger to her lips and chewed her last piece of chicken. "Sorry."

"Mom, it's really not a big deal."

Becca never wanted anyone to leave. She would keep the conversation and food going forever. If they stayed, dessert would be served followed by popcorn followed by probably more popcorn.

Mac wiped his hands with his napkin. "It's okay, Millie. My brother Vince of the GPD is investigating a possible murder, and I am helping out a bit, that's all. I have to question someone at the Christmas Walk. I'd rather not go into too much detail, but yes, helping my brother."

"Oh, wow, is it anyone we know? Anything I can do to help?" Becca took a sip of water.

"No. I can handle it. Just routine cop work is all. Thank you so much for dinner. It was great. I had a wonderful time. Thank you so much." Mac stood up and joined Millie.

"Just a minute." Becca stood and walked into the butler's pantry between the dining room and kitchen.

Millie worried about what Becca might be bringing out of the pantry.

Her mother handed Mac a bag of peanut brittle with red ribbon. "Great to meet you. We will have to do this again very soon. Hopefully we will see you Christmas Day. Millie, oh, I wanted to give you that thing to return to the Tiny Wanderer. Come grab it with me."

"Okay, let's get it."

Mac walked into the foyer to grab his jacket. Millie followed her mother into a back room.

"Mom, what are you doing?" Millie asked.

"Take this with you." Becca pulled a small vial of blue liquid out of a closet.

"Mom...no."

"Millificent Nicole, you will take this. It loosens lips. Helps people tell the truth. Maybe it can help Mac and his brother," Becca insisted.

She'd busted out the full name and middle name. She wasn't messing around. She must like Mac to want to help.

"Okay, Mom. I'll take it. If you insist."

CHAPTER EIGHTEEN

Mac drove Millie to Salem Bank, where Millie's boss had reserved a spot in the parking lot for them to park in. Parking was certainly at a premium especially with the Christmas Walk officially underway. Night had fallen on Geneva, and the seasonal lights created an exciting atmosphere.

"The mayor sent a goon to intimidate you. Whoa. What is our next move?" Millie asked.

"We have to determine whether or not it was the mayor. I mean, I didn't actually see the mayor. The goon mentioned the mayor, and I saw the town car and assumed. Right now, we stick with the original plan and question Fanucci. To see what he knows." Mac pulled into the bank parking lot.

People were everywhere. Downtown Geneva

hopped not unlike Times Square on New Year's Eve, on a much smaller scale, of course.

"You don't think this goon is following us, do you?"

"I would have picked up on it. I think. I mean, I hope. I guess I am a bit rusty." Mac put the car in park then scanned the area around them.

"I am sure all is well, Mac. You would have seen him." Millie looked around too. They were both paranoid.

There was no goon in a big black car anywhere.

Mac looked at Millie and shrugged. They both let out a laugh.

"Let's head to Fanucci's then procure a spot for the tree lighting ceremony." Mac opened his car door then grabbed his cane.

"I did take a look at the Fanucci's accounts, and they certainly have enough money to make Patricia a decent offer." Millie followed Mac.

The restaurant was only a block away, and they were a block east of Third Street and away from most of the crowds.

"Good to know. Hey, thanks for being such a good sport and helping me out." Mac grabbed Millie's hand as they walked.

"No problem. I have to admit, it's kind of exciting."

"I was hoping you didn't think I was nuts and so wanted to be a cop again that I was making something out of nothing with Patricia's death. I just knew something wasn't right," Mac said.

"No, I'm glad I'm able to help. You still have your instincts, and those instincts helped save lives. I did worry a little bit earlier in the day. I will be honest."

"Understandably so. And of all days for this to happen, it's the day we go to your parents' house. They were great by the way. Both of them. Really. Your mom is hilarious, and I loved listening to your dad."

"They are great. I think they liked you." Millie squeezed Mac's hand.

"Good. Good. Okay here we are."

Fanucci's fine dining establishment lay ahead. A line formed out the door as their Christmas Walk reservations filled rather quickly. Mac and Millie did not plan on eating any dinner.

"Excuse me. Excuse me. We are meeting someone who is already sitting down. Thanks," Mac said as he cut to the front of the long line.

Bushy eyebrows stood behind the host desk.

"Michael back yet?"

"Ah, yes. Hold on."

This time Mac flashed his badge, and that made the process much quicker.

"I will get him up here straight away." The young host ran to the back of the bar to the swinging doors.

A tall curly-haired Michael Fanucci walked out with a towel in his hands.

Mac and Millie pushed into the small bar area to get his attention. Lots of couples drank wine and waited for their table.

"Can I help you?" Michael asked.

"Yes, need to ask you a few questions." Mac flashed his badge.

"You aren't a cop. I know every cop in Geneva. I don't have to answer to you. As you can see, I am very busy. It's the Christmas Walk, pal." Michael wiped his hands.

"How much did you offer Patricia for the Tiny Wanderer? Why did she reject your offer? Did you get mad and murder her this morning?" Mac yelled since it was so packed and loud.

Only a few people within a couple feet seemed to hear him, and they just kept drinking their wine.

"What?! Get outta here now. Last warning."

Michael shook his head. He turned around and went back through the swinging doors.

Mac started to follow him but, Millie placed her hand on his chest. "Mac, no. Let me try. Wait out here."

"He is pretty mad. Probably wouldn't be good for you to go back there now."

"Yeah, thanks to you, he's mad. Sometimes a bullish approach isn't the best way. Let me handle this." Millie walked through the swinging doors to the back.

CHAPTER NINETEEN

Millie walked with confidence into the hot kitchen of Fanucci's. There were stainless steel counters, cookware, and appliances everywhere, and a red tile floor to mask all the fallen marinara sauce. A full staff of cooks toiled away at the many orders that needed fulfillment.

"Who are you? Dear God, are you with that idiot wannabe cop? You can't be back here," Michael bellowed.

"Mike, I don't know if you remember me. I played softball with your sister. I'm Millie Paderson." Millie pulled her hand from her jacket pocket, and a fast dissipating cloud of dust billowed. She put her hand out for him to shake.

Michael walked closer and into the dust cloud to

shake her hand. He closed and rubbed his eyes. He opened them back up and didn't shake her hand. "Oh wait, yes, Millie. Sofia's friend. Now I remember. What is going on here? Hang on, let me get a drink of water."

Michael turned away and looked to a nearby sink.

Millie held water in a scotch glass in front of her. "Here you go."

"Oh...how...thanks." Michael grabbed the glass from her and drank it fast.

He downed the water mixed with more of Becca's truth concoction.

"Now, Mike, Patricia passed away this morning. Tell me about your negotiations with her for the Tiny Wanderer."

"Order's up!" a cook yelled to a server.

Michael looked distracted by that but then focused his energy on her. "I made her the best offer I could. I even bested Lacy's offer, but she chose to go with Lacy's because she didn't like the plans I had for the property."

"Which were?"

"I wanted to open up a themed Italian beef quick service restaurant with Gordon Artese, the real estate guy in town. She didn't like that and was supposed to sell to Lacy's today. Is she really dead?"

"Yes, she's really dead. Just seems very suspicious—"

"Stop right there. I have no idea why I am telling you all this. Was I pissed about her turning me down? Yes. Very pissed. I would never murder her. That's ridiculous. Now can I get back to work? I have a restaurant to run on one of the busiest weekends of the year." Michael was very demonstrative and used his hands the whole time he spoke his truth. He then went to take another drink of water only to find the glass disappeared from his hand.

"Thanks for your time, Mike. Say hi to Sofia for me." Millie walked out of the kitchen.

Mac waited at the edge of the bar in a sea of people waiting to be seated in the main dining room.

"What happened?" Mac put out his hands in anticipation.

"He talked."

"How did you get him to talk so quick?"

"Magic." Millie blew right past him to the doors.

Mac followed. "Funny. No, for real. What happened?"

The cold night air hit Millie's face, and she took a

deep breath. "He didn't do it. He admitted frustration but didn't kill Patricia."

"How do you know he wasn't lying?" Mac nearly stumbled with his cane.

"He wasn't lying. His sister was one of my best friends in high school. I trust him. He did give us another lead to follow. We need to find Gordon Artese now."

"Wait. Did you say Gordon?"

"Yes, I did. He's a bigshot realtor around here."

"Patricia's daughter is married to a Gordon. Patricia's home is open tonight for the Walk. Let's head there now!"

CHAPTER TWENTY

Mac called Vince.

"I just left the station, Mac! I gave all the stuff to Charlie Gerner. He is taking over the case as I said would happen earlier," Vince said.

"Vince. Get somebody to pick up Gordon Artese. He is a prime suspect in Patricia's murder. He is a realtor in town."

"I know the guy, and he's marred to the daughter. Ugh. Okay, I will call it in. You can stop now, Mac Attack."

"Thanks, Vince. Do you want to know why? I'll see if he's at the Flaherty house which is still open for the Walk."

"No, I want to go on vacation. I trust you, my

brother. If you say it's Gordo, it's Gordo. I am out. Have a good night." Vince ended the call.

Mac and Millie reached Patricia's block.

The exterior of Patricia's Flaherty's ranch looked as if Clark Griswold had decorated it. So many bright white lights and a long line waiting to tour the home. The main attraction of the Christmas Walk wasn't Third Street. The homes around downtown were specifically decorated and staged for the event so people could experience Christmas by walking into the pictures on a Christmas card or even the cover of a cozy mystery novel or just about every Hallmark Christmas movie ever made. The homes were gorgeous, dripping with charm and holiday magic. As Mac observed earlier, Patricia's home was no exception.

"I will flash my badge and get us to the front of the line." Mac walked with his cane. He'd had a very active day. His leg ached. The doctor said that pain would really never dissipate.

They walked to the front of the line. A family of four waited to tour the house near the door.

Mac flashed his badge. "Just here to relieve my guy doing security in here."

"Oh, no problem." The mother stepped to the side.

Mac and Millie entered the house. There was a line of people that curved to the right and into the living room with the Christmas tree on one side and a vast Christmas village on the other.

Mac walked to the kitchen and beyond into the bedroom area, which had been marked as not part of the house tour with a blue velvet rope. Millie followed close behind.

A toilet flushed through the bathroom door on his left.

"Hey, no one is supposed to be back here. Jeez, I stop to pee for a second," a deep voice grumbled.

Mac and Millie walked to the end of the hall and into a bedroom on the right. It must have been Patricia's room. On the bed was a tan jacket and a leather bowling ball bag.

Mac shut the door and locked it behind them. "I recognize that jacket, Millie. It was the goon from earlier. Check the bag."

The pounding steps of the goon walked the hall towards them.

"Millie, check the bag." Mac stood guard at the door and held the handle tight.

Millie's eyes were wide as she checked. "There must be about forty grand in cash in here."

"Check the jacket. Look for an ID with the name Jerry on it," Mac whispered.

Boom! The goon knocked on the door.

Millie found a wallet. "It's a thick wallet."

"That's because it has a badge in it."

"Hey! Open the door! I am a police officer! You can't be in there!" the goon yelled.

"Clear all the pockets."

"Yep, Officer Jerry Haddonfield is his name. Some receipts. A little blue cap."

"A little blue cap? That cap was for a needle. The needle that killed Patricia!"

"Who? Oh no, is that you, O'Malley? You crippled bigshot cop! Open the damn door or I am breaking it down!"

"Good! Come on in so we can arrest you! You are under arrest for the murder of Patricia Flaherty!" Mac yelled.

The pounding and yelling stopped.

Silence.

Heavy footfalls boomed then rapidly faded down the hall. Some people screamed.

"He's running." Millie stuffed the receipt and needle cap in her pocket.

"Yep, he is. And I can't run," Mac said. "You're up, college athlete."

CHAPTER TWENTY-ONE

Millie ran through the door Mac had opened for her and through the hall of the Flaherty ranch. Millie still owned the stolen base record of her college softball program and her high school. Her quick-twitch muscles proved most effective in the sprint. She made the turn out of the hallway and to the front door.

"He went that way!" a few people in line yelled to Millie and pointed toward Third Street.

"Thank you!" Millie ran across the lawn and across the street.

Surely, his plan was to lose her in the crowds on Third Street. If he made it near the courthouse where people waited for the tree lighting ceremony, he'd be very difficult, if not impossible, to find.

She saw him on Fourth Street behind the Tiny Wanderer. He wore a cream cardigan sweater and jeans. He headed to Third, but she gained on him.

He took an angle run across the street from the Tiny Wanderer and would reach the throngs of people walking Third in seconds.

"Shoot." Millie stopped her run and pulled out Jerry's receipts. She waved her hand. *"Reditus Retorno."*

The receipts flew up into the air then darted in the direction Jerry ran.

Millie followed the receipts.

MAC WALKED out of the house and called Vince.

"Why do I keep answering your calls?"

"Did you get to the Artese residence yet? We found his accomplice. He hired Jerry Haddonfield to kill Patricia Flaherty for forty thousand dollars and who knows what else. Jerry is on the run now, and Millie is after him on foot."

"Jerry, that buffoon! Are you kidding me? Oh hell, I will come get you. Hang tight. Let me call and see if they got Artese yet. This is crazy."

"Thanks, Vince. I'm still at Patricia's."

Mac paced the front of the house. How did Jerry

know to threaten him? Had he been in the house and the reflection in the microwave wasn't an illusion? He looked at the picture in his phone.

No. There was nothing in the reflection. Mac looked to the long line of people and the doorway.

The doorbell. The doorbell had a camera. Gordon and Jerry monitored who went into the house. They knew Mac was snooping around and knew to mention the mayor because of how ridiculous the mayor acted about the entire situation. Patricia didn't like cameras and didn't even have them in the Wanderer, but Gordon must have liked them. Mac wondered how closely they'd monitored him the entire day. Maybe they did follow him throughout the day. The thought ran a chill down his spine.

CHAPTER TWENTY-TWO

Millie realized that the spell worked but would only do her any good if she could regain a visual on Jerry. She ran along the brick-paved road. The receipts raced through the air to return to their owner, and Millie faithfully followed.

The crowd went unorganized from a fine line on the sidewalk to a wide splash of people around the Christmas tree in front of the courthouse. The receipts slowed to graceful float back to their owner.

Millie took a wide left turn near the history museum. Jerry must have slowed down amongst the big crowd that anxiously awaited the visual spectacle of the tree lighting. The receipts made their way through the night air and picked up speed towards Route 38.

Millie power walked through the crowd saying, "Excuse me. Sorry," every two feet.

She made it through the most condensed part of the crowd. Route 38 and the receipts lay ahead.

A burst of light hit her peripheral vision. The crowd roared with applause. The tree lighting had commenced. Millie couldn't even look.

She spotted him.

Jerry hobbled to the road and crossed 38, seeming exhausted. He put his hands on his knees and grabbed for his phone. The receipts floated onto his neck. He grabbed them and ripped them apart.

A black town car rolled up to the corner he stood on.

Millie kicked into high gear. She was cold. Her lungs hurt. But she was close.

Too late.

Jerry hopped in the car and took off.

Millie stopped.

She had another option. She shook her head and coughed from her intense run through the cold. She took out her phone and called for backup.

"Hellooooo." Becca's voice sounded distorted from wind.

"Mom, I need you to help me find—"

"Oh, don't worry. I am already in pursuit. You're welcome!" More wind distorted her Mom's voice.

Millie looked up, and sure enough, she could see in the ambient light from Route 38. Her mother and her golden hair, flying high on a broomstick.

"You followed us!" Millie slapped her forehead.

"Now wait a minute. You know I like to watch the tree lighting on the broom. But yes, I followed you, too. They are heading towards the high school. Call Mac and the police. Tell them now. Should I put a petrified spell on the car now or just wait?"

"Just do it. Do it now!"

"Do not yell at your mother, Millie."

CHAPTER TWENTY-THREE

Vince had the rollers going. The lights on his unmarked squad acted as a beacon for Mac to run to. He hobbled as fast as he could. He reached for the door handle as Vince had already pushed the door open for him.

"Patrol rolled up to the Artese household. Gordon took off in his black town car just a few minutes before we got there. Jerry tipped him off, I would guess. The wife slash daughter is being cooperative. Saying that Gordon has been acting strangely and is basically relieved we are about to arrest him. Everyone is looking for him," Vince said.

"Good. I haven't heard from Mill— Oh wait, here she is now." Mac answered his ringing phone.

"Mac. Jerry was picked up on 38 by a town car

which then broke down near the high school. Meet me there."

"Vince, the high school. Hit the sirens. Millie, we will be right there. Jerry is armed so just wait for us!"

"Okay, I'll be careful. I'll watch where they go next. See you soon."

"Be careful." Mac ended the call.

Vince spoke into the police band. "All units. All units. Converge on the high school. Geneva High School. Suspects are stopped in a black sedan. Near the high school."

A few responses patched in and out.

The sirens blared and pounded Mac's ears.

Vince avoided Third at all costs, drove to Seventh Street, floored it north to 38, and made a hard right onto Logan.

The excitement brought joy to Mac's heart. He missed this. Being a cop was fun.

Then it hit him. No way Millie could have chased Jerry who was picked up by car on foot all the way to the high school. How did she know they were near the high school? Something didn't add up.

"MOM, are they still in the car?" Millie's mother

provided overwatch intel from high in the sky on a broomstick.

"They were in for longer than I thought. I used the petrified spell and bricked the vehicle. The two idiots tried starting it for far too long. Anyway, they got out and ran over to the high school and broke a window on the Logan Avenue side of the school. They must be hiding in the school somewhere. Should I go in and petrify them as well?"

"Mom. No. Let the cops take it from here. We don't want to make anyone suspicious." Millie ran to the high school due north on Mckinley Avenue.

"The tree looks beautiful this year," Becca said.

The wind had died down in the background where Millie assumed she hovered.

Millie shook her head. "I will have the authorities sweep the school for them. Yes, the tree does look nice. Mom, keep your focus on the school to see if they come out."

A police car raced past her, lights and sirens going. Then a fire truck's siren whined not far behind.

"Your dad and I really like Mac by the way. Seems like a good man."

"Thanks, Mom." Millie ended the call then called Mac.

"Millie, how did you know—"

"Mac! They are in the high school somewhere. They entered from the Logan Avenue side of the school through a window they broke. Send everyone there."

"Will do. Will do. Vince, we are going to have to search the high school. They entered from Logan. Thanks, Mills!"

CHAPTER TWENTY-FOUR

The blaring sound of sirens filled the air behind Vince's squad car. Mac looked back and saw the lights of the GPD SUVs that followed close. Mac held the side spotlight of the squad car as they neared the brown brick of the two-story and somewhat sprawling Geneva High School.

Mac aimed the spotlight at the side of the building. The windows were tinted, but the strength of the squad torch did reveal shelves of books. The library. The windows themselves had a longer top section and a smaller bottom section that was able to angle open to let air in. Jerry and Gordon smashed a bottom section open and entered the library.

"Vince, stop here. They broke a window into

what looks like the library." Mac gestured to the windows on the side of the school.

"Yep, there's the town car just in the middle of the street with the doors open. They're scrambling." Vince pulled to the curb right behind the town car.

"All units, set up a perimeter around the school. I want cars near every exit! They entered the building on the Logan side of the building through a window leading into the library. Let's make sure they can't get out." Vince put the radio speaker down and handed Mac a .38 pistol and a torch flashlight.

"I thought we couldn't use these things anymore." Mac pushed the button of his torchlight.

Vince opened the car door. "Not tonight. As long as you don't beat Jerry with it, we're fine."

"Oh, Jerry." Mac felt rage burn within. These two men murdered a good friend. He wanted them to pay, and soon they would.

"You gonna make it through that window?" Vince hopped over the sidewalk and onto the grass near the broken window.

"Very funny. I have a cane. I am not a blimp." Mac followed his brother. He left his cane inside the squad though. The adrenaline coursing through his veins would carry him through.

"No cane?" Vince crouched and examined the broken window with his flashlight.

"I will be fine. Watch the glass. Let's get in there." Mac gripped the side of the window frame, bent down, and put his good leg in first. He entered the library and used his flashlight.

Vince followed him in. They both aimed their flashlights in one hand with their guns pointed in the other. Mac limped a bit, but with vigor, he examined the shelving and rows of books on the right and Vince the left. They cleared the library. Nothing.

"Okay, so they are definitely not in the library. Luckily, a pink floating ghost shushing us isn't in here either," Mac said.

"You are such a nerd, Mac. A movie reference now." Vince shook his head.

"They could be in so many places in here. So many classrooms to sweep. Why trap yourself in here? Something isn't adding up." Mac looked out the window, and a few GPD SUVs were parked on the street with rollers spinning and torchlights aimed at the building. By now, the building had to be surrounded.

MILLIE MADE it to the Logan side of the building,

her breathing labored. She put her hands on her knees. Her phone rang.

A pause for breath. "Hello."

"Millie, I forgot to tell you. I think I may have figured out why they went into the school," Becca said from somewhere high above on a broomstick.

"Okay, Mom. What is it? Just tell me." Millie took a deep breath.

"There are tunnels underneath that used to lead to the old Coultrap Elementary school the city demolished a few years ago. Now it's just a field on Peyton and Logan. If they can't find them in the school, maybe they went down into those?"

"Oh, that's right. I forgot about the tunnels! Thanks, Mom. I'll tell Mac."

"Good thing I dressed warm. It is cold up here. Bye!"

Millie continued her jog along the side windows.

A patrolman yelled, "Stop!"

"It's okay! It's okay! She's with me!" Mac yelled as he exited the library.

"Mac! There's always been an old rumor that there are tunnels underneath the school that lead to a field about a block or two away. They could be in there," Millie said.

A loud engine roared from behind Mac. Millie

pointed to a red pickup truck that emerged from the spot where they'd put the dumpsters on this side of the building. The truck clipped the rear bumper of a GPD SUV and sped down Logan, then jumped the curb into the park that held the tennis courts, softball fields, and football field.

"That could be them!" Millie yelled.

"We should check the tunnels, Millie. Vince, get after that pickup truck!" Mac yelled.

Vince ran to his unmarked squad. Two GPD cars were already in pursuit of the red truck.

CHAPTER TWENTY-FIVE

Mac and Millie entered the library through the broken window. This time, Mac walked over and turned the lights on.

"Okay, so how do we get to these tunnels?" Mac asked.

Millie walked out into the hall. "This is the older side of the building, hence the musty smell. If we hang a right out of the library and continue down this hallway, the E hallway, we should be able to find a door to a basement and to the tunnels."

Mac shined the flashlight into the dark hallway. Glints of metal from the students' locks filled his vision. He limped but kept pace with Millie.

"You sure you are okay without your cane, Mac?"

"I am so jacked up with adrenaline right now, I am feeling no pain." The light from his torch bobbed up and down. Nothing but linoleum flooring and student lockers lined the hallway. Ahead was another entryway of tinted doors and windows marked 10S. To the left of the entrance, a door lay open to a stairwell that led down.

"This has to be it." Millie pointed to the open door.

"Be careful, Mills." Mac reached Millie and opened the door all the way. He noticed a light switch and hit it. The stairwell had one tube light above that blinked to full power. The musty smell grew stronger upon entry. Mac and Millie made their way down a few steps before they noticed a gravel and dirt floor below.

"Gotta be a tunnel," Mac said.

"This is not at all creepy. Hunting for killers in a creepy underground tunnel from hell." Millie shrugged her shoulders.

Mac's phone buzzed in his pants pocket. Vince.

"Hello, did you get the truck? Did you catch them?"

"No. We didn't get them. They are clever though. They paid the janitor a thousand large in cash to provide a distraction, which means they are probably in those tunnels."

"Millie said she thought the tunnels lead to a field where Coultrap Elementary used to be? Head there but still keep everyone else on the perimeter of the school."

"Will do. I'll head there in case they pop out of the field. I think the Viking ship is there now. Geneva High's mascot is Vikings and a replica of a Viking ship is on display there but under a tent."

"A Viking ship?! Cool!" Mac yelled then covered his mouth for fear of Jerry and Gordon in possible close proximity.

"Be careful down there. Bye." Vince ended the call.

"Well, you aren't gonna believe this. They are probably in this tunnel. The truck was just a distraction. They paid a janitor to take off and draw us away," Mac said.

"Wonderful. You first," Millie said.

"Gee, thanks." Mac descended the last few steps to the dirt and gravel floor of the tunnel. He shined a light down it. It looked more like a coal mine shaft than a tunnel. The walls were not bored out into a circular shape. Rickety planks and wooden pillars held the weight of the surrounding soil above and around them.

Mac and Millie walked into the tunnel of doom. Every few feet, audible cracking of wood filled the air. Mac's flashlight still bobbed up and down with his limp. Every so often a rat would scurry about on the ground then find a way into holes within the tunnel walls.

"Oh, gross. That's not unsettling at all." Millie shook her head.

"They must have got the key from the janitor they paid off. I can't believe this is still open. The school is lucky kids haven't found this." Mac took a deep breath. The longer they walked, the more his leg hurt. Adrenaline's effect waned.

"How much longer do you think this tunnel goes, Millie?"

"I don't think it can be that much longer to the field."

A loud boom emanated from the direction they walked, followed by a smacking sound next to Mac's right ear. Splinters of wood showered his head and shoulder. "Get down, Millie! We are being shot at!" Mac hit the ground and turned the flashlight off.

"Oh!" Millie hit the ground next to Mac.

"Cover your ears." Mac squeezed off two return shots with the .38 his brother gave him.

"Are they gone?" Millie asked with a muffled tone.

"I don't know. They must have been just out of the range of the flashlight's beam. I'm going to crawl about twenty feet or so then turn it back on and shoot if I need to. Just stay put."

"Be careful."

Mac army crawled as best he could and dealt with the pain in his leg. Luckily, no rats squeaked around him.

He made considerable distance about twenty-five paces. He raised to one knee. Took a deep breath. Aimed the gun and moved his thumb to power on his torch.

He closed his eyes. Took another deep breath. Eyes opened, he turned the flashlight back on.

An empty tunnel lay ahead, complete with doorway with a stairwell to the surface. Mac turned and signaled to Millie.

Millie ran to him. "Where did they go? End of the line, huh?"

They walked to the doorway and the steps that were caked with dirt and grass. Jerry and Gordon had found the way out. They climbed the stairs. Fresh air filled Mac's lungs.

"This is it. This is the field. The Viking ship is in there." Millie pointed to the large half-cylinder tent.

Vince ran over to their position in front of the tent. "Mac! Gordon has decided to hole himself up in the tent and take Jerry hostage."

"He took a shot at us in the tunnel," Mac said.

"He saw me and panicked. Grabbed Jerry," Vince said.

"I will cover the back of the tent. You guys take the front." Millie ran to the opposite side of the tent.

"Get away or Jerry dies!" Gordon screamed from inside the tent.

CHAPTER TWENTY-SIX

Most criminals tend to do stupid things at the risk of possibly getting caught, yet Gordon and Jerry tried to stray from the norm with the pickup truck stunt but ultimately ended up trapped. Vince had already redirected units to the tent in the field where Coultrap Elementary used to be.

"Gordon! Why don't you just give this up? Come on out!" Vince yelled.

Six squad cars surrounded the tent. Twelve cops shined their spotlights and headlights at it.

"You have nowhere to go!" Mac yelled.

A gunshot rang out from inside the tent.

Vince and Mac took cover behind Vince's squad car.

Another gunshot. This time, Jerry came running out of the tent with his hands up.

"He's nuts. He's lost it!" Jerry yelled.

Another shot hit Jerry. He fell on the grass hard a few feet from Vince's squad. A shoulder wound, a big and nasty one at that.

"Jerry! Jerry! What kind of gun you got? It sounds big," Vince said.

Jerry mumbled something.

"Jerry, you need to repeat what you said. Don't mumble this time," Mac yelled.

"A .44!"

"Okay so he only has two more shots," Vince said.

"Gordon! Come out with your hands up. You have two bullets, and we all have a lot more bullets out here. Your odds aren't great," Mac yelled.

Snow started to fall. Lots and lots of snow. The wind picked up. It went from zero weather to a blizzard in about five seconds.

"What is happening?" Mac asked.

"I BROUGHT your wand just in case." Becca dropped the magical thin stick into Millie's palm from above.

"Thanks, Mom."

Millie used the weather to her advantage. She stood far enough back from the tent and in a resident's yard across Peyton Street to avoid detection and wielded her wand with confidence. A wind spell did the trick. She swirled the wand with steady repetition. The temporary structure that covered the Viking ship gave way. The ties and rope that fastened the tent to the ground loosened and whipped around. The tent acted as a sail and blew away to the school parking lot.

THE WIND DIED DOWN. The snow fell gently. Gordon shivered next to the wooden Viking longboat. Circular wooden shields and oars surrounded him as if he were going to use them somehow. He cracked.

"Drop it." Mac pointed his torch and .38 at the murderer.

"Gordon. Enough. Drop the gun!" Vince followed his brother, gun aimed.

Twelve other police officers aimed their sidearms at the murderer.

The well-dressed criminal dropped the large .44 Magnum hand cannon.

CHAPTER TWENTY-SEVEN

Mac, Millie, and Vince sat at a table in the Geneva Police station.

"In order to make sure his deal to partner with Michael on a possible fast food franchise went through, he murdered his own mother-in-law to prevent her from making the purchase with Lacy's. Or should I say he had Jerry do the actual dirty work. Jerry had a needle cover in his pocket of the jacket he wore when he tried to intimidate me off the case which explains the bruise on the victim's neck. Patricia found out from Michael that his intentions for the property was a more upscale fast food restaurant, and she decided to go with the lesser offer from Lacy's. Lacy's was going to preserve the building, even the staff, and manage the lucrative property.

Yes, there may have been a Lacy's logo somewhere on the sign, but the building and employees would be safe," Mac said.

"What about the 40k in Jerry's bowling bag?" Vince asked.

"Suzy has just confirmed that her mother was planning on getting a property in Naples, Florida to retire. Her courteous son-in-law needed a forty-thousand dollar down payment on a property she wanted. When Gordon realized Patricia valued more things in her life than just the maximum amount of money, like her employees and family-built Tiny Wanderer, he decided not to make that down payment for her and use the cash to pay Jerry for the big hit."

"That is cheap for a hit. Isn't it? These days? You said Jerry tried to intimidate you?" Vince said while jotting down more notes.

"Yes, he did. They did not account for a retired, physically limited cop to walk in the house this morning. The timing was carefully maximized to make any possible investigation be put to the wayside, or in this case, no investigation would happen because she was so old and thus, you know, heart attack. Jerry pulled the needle out quickly and never applied any pressure afterwards to prevent bruising on her neck. He gently laid her on the floor.

I don't know, maybe Jerry felt bad after murdering a little old lady as there were no signs of a fall. No bumps. No bruises."

"Back to the intimidation question, Mac. Focus."

"Oh, oh, sorry. Yes, about the timing. Gordon works closely with the mayor at times and frequents city hall and Chamber of Commerce meetings as Suzy has also just confirmed. Well, he knew the day of the Christmas Walk that the mayor would want to sweep any tragedy under the rug for the preservation of tradition and economic stability. Gordon was exactly right. The mayor panicked and tried to hush-hush everyone. Even you, Vince. Luckily you snapped out of it and did do some work."

"Millie, how do you deal with this? He can't answer the question about intimidation. He can't focus." Vince laughed.

"I am getting to that. The doorbell camera. Not only was Jerry still in the house when we first saw the body together, Vince, so he saw me then. But also, again when I entered the house to take some pictures, which I am pretty sure now, Mills, that Jerry was in the house with me when I was taking pictures and was in the reflection on the microwave. They also knew I was in the house again because..."

"Doorbell camera."

"Yes, Gordon even pretended I wasn't in the house, but he knew. No need to do anything about me because that would be an admission of guilt. As the day wore on, though, I kept turning up places they didn't want me like Fanucci's. Heck, maybe they even knew we went to the Hennington, Millie. Oh, and does the mayor own a town car as well?"

Vince rubbed his temple. "He uses Pick Up Plus Premium to drive him around town. A rideshare service. He is that ridiculous."

"Oh, so Gordon and the Pick Up Plus Premium driver just have similar tastes in cars because Jerry got into a town car in front of Fanucci's after he tried to intimidate me off the case. Which again proves how much of an opportunist Gordon is. Use the mayor's similar car and the mayor himself to get me off the scent."

"That about cover it? Can I go on vacation now?" Vince asked.

"I think so." Mac looked at Millie. "Can we go to the Christmas Walk now?"

CHAPTER TWENTY-EIGHT

Mac and Millie walked down Third Street together south from Route 38. The crowds dissipated. A few of the restaurants and bars had people in them, and no one was outside. Too cold. The snow steadily fell and started to leave an accumulation of sparkling perfection on the ground and the branches of the beautiful, bright, and grand Geneva Christmas tree.

"Epic fail on actually enjoying the Christmas Walk this year," Millie said.

"Yes, what a day. What a crazy day. Best part was that I got to spend it with you. Again, your parents are great. You are great." Mac stopped in front of the tree.

"You are pretty great yourself, Officer O'Malley." Millie smiled.

"I really mean it you are wonderful and I have been feeling a certain way for quite awhile now and well, I am in love with you, Millie." Mac's eyes twinkled just like the lights of the grand Christmas tree they stood aside.

"I love you too, Mac." Millie embraced him.

They shared a kiss while snowflakes danced around them in the warm glow of the Christmas lights.

Mac pulled his head back. "Now that we are making declarations, there is just a couple things that are bothering me. Inexplicable things. How did you get Michael to talk so quickly? Also, how did you follow a speeding car all the way to the high school on foot? I mean, I know you are fast and have all the records but..."

"All the records. I have *all* the records." Millie laughed.

"How did you do it? Seriously, tell me."

"Um." Millie looked at him and raised her eyebrows.

Mac smiled. "How am I to go on when the person I am madly in love with won't tell me things?!"

The snow fell. The light from the Christmas tree made her face glow with the spirit of the season, of love, of togetherness, of magic.

"Well, the man I happen to be madly in love with will need to deal with the fact that I am a—"

"You are a what?" Mac's eyebrow raised.

"I am a witch. I used magic to get Michael to talk so quickly and Mom may have been watching overhead while flying on a broom following Gordon and Jerry. That did happen. That going to be okay with you? Or? Can we just get a drink now?" Mille rubbed Mac's shoulders.

Mac's eyes were wide. Utter shock permeated from his face to Millie who kept rubbing his shoulders in comfort.

"Wait a minute...my girlfriend is magical. Like legit magical?! This is amazing!" Mac yelled.

"Shh! Let's keep it down a bit." Millie laughed.

"We are going to solve so many more mysteries with my instincts and your magic. Magical mystery solving dynamic duo!" Mac yelled again.

"Mac! Shush! Let's just get a drink."

"Can we fly on a broomstick to the bar? Please?"

Millie shook her head and laughed.

THE END

"Millie has requested that I formally query you for your opinion of this crazy day in December in the form of a book review. So please leave a review of "The Christmas Walk Caper." We thank you very much.

MAC, NON-WRITER AND RETIRED CHICAGO COP.

So I have another entire series! (Actually two other series, more on that later.) I consider it some of my most original work and you just haven't quite experienced a Holiday story quite like this one. Please enjoy three three-chapter excerpts from the Readers' Favorite Gold, Silver, and Bronze medal-winning book series- "The Tannenbaum Tailors"-tiny tree elves and fairies that take care of Christmas trees around the world!

29

INTERRUPTED SLEEP (EXCERPT FROM 'A CAPITOL ABDUCTION')

Jane's wings ached. She flapped her wings repeatedly hoping to work out the sting. The damage from the South Pole's wind pervaded her every thought, emotion, movement. The events of the past Christmas might have changed her forever. A fairy's wings are a fairy's identity. She hoped that with wing therapy and exercises the pain would lessen over time.

She didn't have time for pain.

The Fae Flyer's pride lay in her ability to lead, to command, to fly among her fellow Fae with a sense of confidence that pushed her to being one promotion away from Admiral.

She stood in front of her bathroom mirror. Jane removed her leather aviator helmet and pushed her fingers through her hair and rubbed her scalp. Her blond hair was a knotted, curly mess. She sighed blowing her hair from her face with an overlapped bottom lip and jutted chin. She examined her dirty, rosy-blemished face. Jane sighed again.

Exhaustion weighed on her like a ton of bricks. Missions like the one she just flew having thwarted another Spiritless assault had sapped her strength.

It was time to rest.

Jane couldn't find the energy to shower. She took off her jacket and sat down on the sink to remove her boots. She kicked off the right and struggled with the left one. Her hammock looked like heaven. Jane slipped off the sink and fell on her butt.

"Ugh. Just what I needed. Nice work, Jane. Nice. Work."

She sat on the floor and pushed the boot off then dragged herself over to the hammock, folded her wings and lay down. Within seconds she was out.

The vibration of her phone rattled on her desk. The phone's silent but physically obnoxious function caused it to fall off her desk and onto the floor, where it still shook.

Jane's eyes cracked open.

"Ugh! I just fell asleep!" The fairy grabbed for

her phone still in her hammock. She swung herself to the phone and picked it up.

"Hello..."

"Jane. I need you come down to the hangar," a male voice burst from the speaker.

"I was just there...what could have possibly happened? I just fell asleep." Jane rubbed her forehead.

"Jane it's been about 14 hours since you left here. I need you back here now, that's an order."

"Yes, sir. Right away." Jane ended the call. Admiral Pixie's tone was far too serious and panicked. He was her commanding officer, but he usually acted so casual and aloof that it frustrated her. Something must have rattled him. Jane rolled herself out her hammock and stretched her wings, then went back to rubbing her head. Her headache was bad, not a full migraine but close enough. Her bottle of DUST was depleted. She took too much of it anyway. She will have to deal with the bad headache and the fatigue of perhaps, sleeping too long.

Jane walked over to the mirror and quickly put her hair up in a ponytail. She splashed her face with some cold water, secured her helmet and boots and was off.

30

FAILURE TO REPORT

Jane's wings still stung from her last adventure. She flew a little slower to lessen the pain and enjoy the journey. The Fairies' Hollow was just outside the North Pole's residential trees where the tree elves lived. She flew through a tunnel of ice and tree bark that were lit up by tracking lights all the way to the outside. The round bulbs were colored blue and yellow and they gently flashed, as to provide a sense of peace for the Fae who lived in North Pole Hollow. Jane reached the tunnel's end. The view still took her breath away, even after flying out of it her whole life. The North Pole's residential pine trees blinked and beamed with the colors of the rainbow.

The tree elves really know how to decorate their ornamental homes, each tree with a different combination of two colors. Jane passed the Western tree's orange and red lights and ahead was the North Tree's blue and gold bulbs. The smaller residential trees surrounded the massive, majestic, Home Tree: the official Tannenbaum Tailor headquarters for tree elves that maintain Christmas trees in human homes every year.

Beyond the grand circle of Christmas trees is North Pole City. The supreme craftsmanship and immersive detail made the North Pole's buildings incredible. The Workshop's multi-colored and ever-changing spectrum of colors was a sight to see and representative of the work always being done inside its hallowed halls: toy research and development, new decorative technologies, all refined and inno-vated to raise and maintain Christmas spirit levels.

Everything had a purpose. Every building's architecture conveyed a message. The only exception was the hangar to the outside of the city center, where the fairies worked alongside Tannenbaum Tailor pilots and their Icicle ships. It was just a massive half-cylinder and was purely functional. Jane sighed. She could have used a few days away from work.

She flew into the hangar bay. The maintenance teams were flying around, touching up the Tannenbaum Tailors' Icicle ships. All around Jane hover engines fired. The noise was loud, and it did not help Jane's headache. Her head pounded. She winced and pulled her leather helmet down farther. Its cushion was no match for the decibels of noise.

Pixie's office was elevated over the rest of the hangar bay. Jane landed on the catwalk and could see him sitting and looking out the window. He must have sensed her presence and stood to greet her.

"Someone's eager to see me." Jane landed on the catwalk next to Pixie's office.

Pixie opened his door, "Come in and have a seat."

Jane sunk into the cushy comfortable office chair.

"Okay what's going on? Anyone else going to join us or no?"

"Right now, I think its best we keep this to ourselves and then we can decide who else we want to include. Most of the Tailor Icicles have returned or are accounted for. All the Flyers have reported in as well, with the exception of three Fairies. Three Tailor teams have reported their flyer's disappearance."

Jane took her helmet off and leaned forward in the chair. Pixie paced behind his desk.

"So, three fairies have disappeared?! Are they

connected in some way? Where were their mission areas?" Jane asked.

"Yes, they were all on duty in the Washington, D.C. metro area. Now they are gone. I brought you in because you are my best flyer. D.C. is the most surveilled city in America. I can't send the entire fleet to search but we can't have fairies flying all over the nation's capital. I need you to find them and bring them home." Pixie put his hands on his desk and gave a worried look to Jane. She could see the tired lines around his eyes. He hadn't slept. She felt guilty about the 14 hours of sleep she just enjoyed.

Jane straightened up in her chair.

"Yes, sir."

31

DETAIL AND DETAIL

"With the attempted Spiritless invasion of the NP, the Home Tree's communications were shut down, the Tailor teams attempted to report the missing Fae after they exhausted their search for them in their respective assigned trees and human homes." Pixie examined the report in the middle of his desk, glasses balanced on the end of his nose.

"They came back to make the reports and their trees were probably taken down. It's their protocol. I understand that." Jane leaned over to look at the report as well.

"The Tailor teams who reported were devastated and worried. They are overwhelmed with news of the thwarted Spiritless invasion. Still you should pay them all a visit," Pixie said.

"The timeline is interesting. A fairy goes missing on December 23rd, then two in rapid succession on the 25th," Jane said.

"That is really all we know at this point. I would suggest recruiting another flyer to accompany you on the investigation."

"I have someone in mind already. I just hope she isn't as sore as I am."

"I will have the Tailor teams here for further questioning when you get back." Pixie said.

"COCO, YOU HOME?" Jane knocked on Coco's round door in North Pole Hollow.

No answer.

Jane knocked again, a little harder this time. Jane noticed a light turn on in through the small window in the door.

"Hold on...ouch...ugh." Coco's dark brown hair covered most of her face. She attempted to brush it back as she opened her door slowly.

"Are you as exhausted as I am?" Jane asked, happy to see her fellow Fae Flyer.

"I think I may be more... I just used the power Frenetic to and from the Spiritless' South Pole lair in the last week." Coco chuckled.

Jane felt the instinct to act as Coco's superior officer but, instead hugged her dear friend.

"Thank you so much for braving the journey. Without you, the North Pole would be lost." Jane's eyes teared up as she held Coco close.

"It was my duty. I was just doing my job. Ouch."

"Oh gosh! Sorry I know you are sore!" Jane finally let go.

"I am so sorry to bother you, but we have a problem and if you are physically able, I could use your help, actually, three fairies and their families could use your help."

Coco looked at her bandaged burned wing. A firework display from a human theme park had injured the wing on her journey back to the North Pole.

"I should be good to go."

A Capitol Abduction AVAILABLE NOW

32

OFF- TREE (EXCERPT FROM 'THE SECRET SNOWBALL')

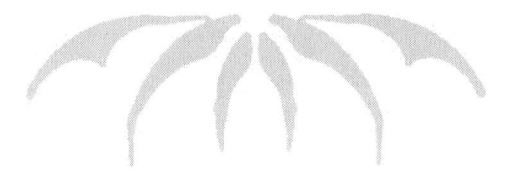

On his way to the lower branches, Brendan ran into Tonto on his way to check the water levels in the tree stand. He saw his Captain rappelling faster and faster down to the stand.

"Captain! Where you headed in such a hurry?" Tonto asked.

Tonto was far too bright to buy any lie Brendan would tell. The new Captain was a bad liar anyway. Tonto was talented, came from a long line of quality tree elves, great Tailors. He would be Captain of his own tree one day for sure.

Brendan just came out with it, "I am going off tree to ask the boy for help."

"What? Captain! You aren't serious are you?" Tonto grabbed his arms and looked into his eyes.

Brendan shrugged him off.

"Under purview of the Tailor Code, given certain situations emergency powers are granted to the Captain of the team to, within reason, use whatever means necessary to accomplish the mission and uphold the oath the Tailors take when they graduate from the academy. This is how I see it," Brendan said.

"Going off-tree and breaking the Silence Protocol is a bit much, perhaps too much power, don't you think? Not to mention dangerous! What would Captain Mas do?" Tonto said.

"Tonto, you make a whole lot of sense but, I am the Captain now. Normally I would not think of doing anything like this but if this tree is taken down, if the Snowball is exposed, if we fail...then Christmas is over."

"There has to be another way! The Tailors Code forbids that you do this. The Silence Protocol takes precedence! How do you know if that kid, who looks like he might almost be a teenager and probably doesn't believe in Santa anymore, will not crush you when he sees you? Or worse, capture you and spread the news that we exist?" Tonto said.

"I don't know. But it is worth a shot." He hooked his Glimmerlift to the bottom branch and descended to the tree skirt. "Tonto take care of the tree while I am gone."

Tonto just shook his head and glimmerlifted up the tree. Tonto had a very literal interpretation of the Tailor Code. He is next in line to become Captain and follows the rules to the letter. Ever since his parents died while on a mission, he never takes any chances. Perhaps the burden of leadership will change his mind one day.

Brendan was alone among mountains of wrapped presents. He walked towards the edge of the tree skirt. Nerves rattled. Sweat gleamed from his forehead. He took his hat off for a moment and wiped his brow with his right arm.

"One minuscule step for me, one giant leap for elvenkind."

Brendan stepped down into the fibers of the carpet and headed towards the stairs. He knew the general direction he had to go. If he needed a refresher he would jump.

The fibers were like tall grass, tall enough to obscure his vision. He fastened his Glimmerlight goggles to the back of his head and clicked them on. The family was asleep so he hoped for no interference to the stairs, leading to the bedroom. He leaped to find his way. He saw a big black blob in between him and his destination. The human's poufy dog lay before him...sleeping. At least he hoped.

"I am so tiny and stealthy. No problems just go around the big dog," Brendan thought

He continued through the fibers of the carpet, on a path that would bring him around the dog. A toy with a hole in it lay next to the dog, probably laced with peanut butter or something. "I think they called those congs? Fitting since the dog is as big as King Kong to me."

He moved around the dog successfully. The dog slept. Nothing but breathing could be heard. The dog lay in front of the stairs he needed to ascend. Luckily, Brendan had his trusty Glimmerlift with him! He aimed towards the side railing a couple feet above the dog. His Glimmerlight goggles aided him as he aimed toward the rail's underside.

"GRRRRRR....." a growl sounded to his right.

He thought about taking the shot and zipping away. Instead, he found himself in a staring contest with two black eyes framing a long, snarled snout. The staring was really not a game he entered into voluntarily. "Elves must smell differently?" Brendan tried to figure out a good reason why the dog woke up and how he was going to get away from the giant, poufy, rather angry canine at that.

"Coal," Brendan said, cursing.

33

PLAY TIME

The dog's breath hit him like the winds preceding an arctic twister. Except the wind was hot and smelled of something the dog should not be eating nor any living creature for that matter. The growls ceased and then a giant white paw came crashing down! Brendan rolled out of the way, with his Glimmerlift still at the ready in his right hand. He shot towards the dog's cong. The line tightened, the hook fastened inside the dog's toy and he zipped right in.

The inside of the dog's cong smelled like peanuts and it was a bit slimy from leftover peanut butter and probably the...Yep the dog's tongue slithered into the cong. He pressed himself up against the back of the cong. Brendan's head and body shook as the cong turned and tumbled as the dog's paw secured it to the floor. He pressed his body against the wall. He felt the heat of the dog's breath again. The tongue lathered the tip of his shoe and then retreated.

Brendan almost let a breath of relief out when he slid from the back of the inside of the cong to the opening in the front in a flash! Peanut butter stuck to his face. He grabbed the side of the opening tight as the toy shook and jolted up and down. The inside of the cong contracted as the dog's jaw bit down on it. Luckily the dog's jaw muscles weren't that of a larger, more ferocious canine, otherwise, the tiny tree elf would have been smashed. The dog thrashed more. Brendan's grip loosened. The dog's strategy was working. His legs moved closer to the opening where his hands held on! His body was shifting to the side. One more thrash and he would be hanging out of the cong. Too close to the dog's sharp teeth.

"GRRRR!" The dog threw the cong with Brendan now dangling from the opening back towards the tree, well away from the stairs. Brendan let go of the cong. He flew through the air like Jane, except soon he would be falling.

He aimed the Glimmerlift at a wooden table against the wall, across from the tree. He took a shot, the force of the dog's throw depleted. He began to fall. The line from the Glimmerlift seemed to move in slow motion. His little elf body would not take a fall from this height well. "Oh, coal!" He cursed. "Coal! Coal! Coal!"

34

COME TO THE STABLE

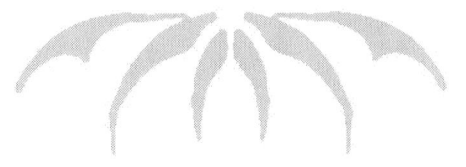

"Oh, for the love..." The line from the Glimmerlift tightened a few inches from the carpet. Brendan zipped up to the top of the wooden table into some fluffy decorative cotton, used to resemble snow. He rolled around in the fluff, giggled, and yelled, "I love my glimmerlift! I love you! I love you!" He even gave it a kiss as he fastened the hook back to his belt.

The Tailor Captain stood up and surveyed the table top. Statues of Santa, gingerbread houses, snowmen, ice skaters, and miniature pine trees combined for a wonderful Christmas display. He bet it looked even better when the twinkle lights were plugged in. As he walked on the fluff, he felt underneath the fake snow, lights used to illuminate such a quaint, literally quaint, Christmas village. At the back corner of the table was a dark building. Captain Brendan guessed it had to be the stable with the Baby Jesus on display. His Glimmerlight goggles helped him find a way through the statues and trees to the stable.

The baby lay peacefully in his manger. His mother and father close to him, watching in awe at their newest and greatest gift. The three wise men stood with the finest gifts of the ancient world. Their only compass, the North Star, reminded Brendan of his current objective. He had to make it to the boy's room. Christmas must go on. The moments such as the one on display here, the celebration of a child's birth must endure.

He looked to the top of the stable and realized he might be able to glimmerlift along the twinkle lights hanging from the windows on the wall behind the stable to the stairs. He'd be far away from the carpet and the dog. He aimed his Glimmerlift to the roof of the stable when the lights under the fluff turned on! He quickly ran behind the Baby Jesus. If the lights were turned on, a human must be close!

THE SECRET SNOWBALL AVAILABLE NOW

35

SEIZURE (EXCERPT FROM 'BRETHREN OF THE SAINTS')

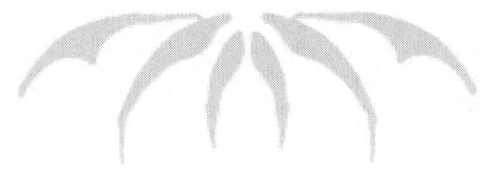

Lily checked the spirit levels and vitality of the tree, something she hadn't done in a while due to all the other more pressing situations. They checked out just fine, thankfully. She checked in with Billy, Steve, and Tonto, who were all at different sections of the tree double-checking for Brendan. As she pressed her com to get another status report from Irene, she felt a cold hand grasp her neck.

"You will do as I say or be silenced forever." The mysterious intruder spun her around to greet her face to face. A blue-grey skinned elf dressed in black with dark sunglasses and a crooked nose stood with eleven dark elves behind him.

"Hello, Lillian. You will help us out a great deal in the next few hours."

"Spiritless...What have you done with the Captain?" Lily managed to speak despite the hand around her neck.

"Ah your Captain is the least of your concerns right now. You will do what I say. If you refuse, then you will never see your Captain again."

"Let me go!" Lily managed a stern voice.

The Head Spiritless elf eased his grip.

"The first order of business will be to close all internal coms. I want your Tailors to only have the ability to communicate with you."

Lily closed the coms and a tear welled up in her left eye.

"Next, you will order each of them to go to a separate specific part of the tree, that you think Brendan might be there or ask them to do a normal check related to their individual duties. You decide. Be convincing. Or else."

"You want me to lure them into traps?"

"I knew I could count on you."

He made hand signals and the eleven Spiritless split into four groups. Three groups of three males and one pair composed of a male and female. The groups left the command center, in a swift and orderly fashion.

"Let's get the day after Christmas started right,"

the Head Spiritless said as the faint light of dawn hit the tree through the windows in the house.

36

TAILOR TRAPS

"I want your Ornament Tailor up here at the top of the tree," the Head Spiritless said.

"Billy. Come in. Over," Lily called.

"Yep. Go ahead, Lily. Over," Billy answered.

"Could you please check the Icicle on the back of the tree? I think the loading ramp may still be open?"

"Yes, ma'am, still no sign of Brendan. Out."

"Now, your Water and Needle Tailor, Tonto, I want him in the middle towards the trunk and the Fire Tailor at the bottom. I understand Irene is currently fighting our termites. No worries about her just yet," the Head Spiritless said.

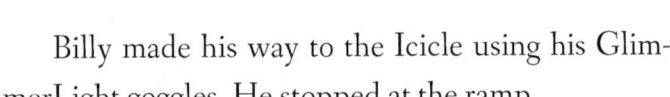

Billy made his way to the Icicle using his Glim-merLight goggles. He stopped at the ramp.

"Hey Steve. Come in. I could use your muscles with this ramp. Over."

No response.

"Steve. Come in. Over."

Still nothing.

"Hey Lily, I can't get a hold of Steve. Can you reach him? Over?"

"The network is down at the moment. You can only reach me here at tree top. Over."

About to respond, Billy saw a blinding flash. He felt a hard blow to his head and another before he fell unconscious onto the ramp of the Icicle transport.

Tonto checked the trunk on the middle branches.

"Hey Lily, these branches and needles seem strong."

A flash. Tonto fell to his knees. He attempted to rip off his goggles when a Spiritless elf kneed him in the face. Two others grabbed him from behind. Tonto fought to get up and nearly pushed the two off his back. The one at his front forced a hood over his head and punched him twice in the face. The two behind him secured him with tinsel. Tonto struggled to break free, but couldn't move.

Steve checked the hoses and hydrants at the bottom of the tree. He then went down to the tree stand to check the water levels. He reached the stand when he felt a kick at his back and fell into the water. He looked up. Three Spiritless elves stood at different spots, in a circle around him. He heard one say, "Release!" The three elves dropped tinsel ropes. A large, heavy ornament fell on Steve, who was treading water, and knocked him out.

"Tailors are secured, sir. Just the one female remains. Over," reported a Spiritless from somewhere in the tree.

"Very good. We have a plan for the female if she makes it out of the tunnels."

Lily cringed and shook her head in despair.

SHAKE THE FOUNDATION

Irene blasted the seemingly never ending wall of termites that made it within centimeters of her. She had already used three flares to keep them back and hoped that the extinguisher wouldn't run out of carbon dioxide. She had been laying on the spout for the last fifteen minutes. The line of termites finally thinned out. She froze the last one. Now she had the task of clearing all the frozen bugs out of the way to reach the cement foundation. The bugs must have found some cracks in the cement to get through from the outside.

The termites were ugly, with sharp pincers jutting out from the sides of their gaping mouths. Even dead ones still seemed threatening. Irene coughed at all the CO_2 hanging in the heavy air of the tunnel. She had to weave her way in between and over all the termites that lay in front of her. Irene could see the end of the tunnel. The corner wall and the cement foundation inched ever closer.

The Lighting Tailor made it to the end of the mud tunnel to find a steep, sloped drop. She shined her flashlight down the incline. The foundation looked craggy and treacherous in spots. The descent into the cement slab, under Jack's house, proved considerably more tight and slick than the first part of the tunnel. Irene slipped and fell a few centimeters.

Her biggest concern was the fire extinguisher. If it hit a jagged spot in the crack of the cement it could leak, explode, and possibly kill her. Irene slid slowly now as if on a water slide- the kind where one has to lay down and cross one's hands across one's chest. All of a sudden, she sped up and could hear the metal of the extinguisher clanging off bumps in the cement. She couldn't stop.

With her eyes closed, she felt her speed lessen and mud in between her fingers. The collection of mud in her fingers provided a smooth stop and prompted a sigh of relief, Irene opened her eyes. Darkness enveloped her. GlimmerLight goggles would be useful at the moment, but the moisture of the tunnel would have ruined them. She had three flares left. The flashlight weakened. Her extinguisher was running low. She hoped the nest was close. Luckily, the tank had only suffered minor scratches and a tiny dent.

Irene popped a flare. She began to crawl into another horizontal mud tunnel and secured the flashlight to her belt. She forgot to call Lily with a status report and then remembered that communication was impossible this deep underground. Irene was truly alone.

This last tunnel ran under the lawn of the house and directly to the nest. Irene army-crawled toward it. She could sense a slight difference in the way the air felt in this tunnel, slightly cooler, and fresh. A new wall of termites blocked the entrance to the nest. They were the workers, the fierce defenders. Irene had had enough and crawled right up to them spraying sporadically. She heard their high-pitched squeals. The ones that crawled underneath their frozen brothers, she stabbed with the hook of her GlimmerLift.

One of the pincers from a worker termite caught her sleeve! She slammed the termite into the side of the mud tunnel, splattering termite juice onto her arm and shoulder. She pushed out of the pile and into the nest where there was enough room to stand up. Irene let loose another flare and threw it into the middle of the nest, illuminating the mother termite. A long, disgusting, pale, slimy, pulsating abdomen made up her womb. Her body was much bigger than her babies and her head was much taller than that of her brood. The tiny Tailor would have been intimidated earlier, but not now.

Irene kept the other worker termites back with the light. She had a plan. She removed the fire extinguisher from her back and threw it at pulsating abdomen of the mother termite. Still holding the flare, she backed up to the entrance of the nest. A worker tripped her. More termites swarmed to her on the ground. With no fire extinguisher, she would have to use her own brute force. She peeled one off her chest that had been biting at her face. The mother termite shrieked loudly, urging her crew to kill.

Irene managed to get back on her feet. Flare still illuminated, she jabbed the light into the next closest termite, and its insides glowed. She tossed the flare to the side and beat the rest with her GlimmerLift. With more closing in, she aimed the business end of the GlimmerLift at the fire extinguisher next to Mama Termite and shot. The hook sped and sunk into the metal of the tank. Carbon dioxide spewed out of it blanketing the mother's abdomen. The shriek turned shrill. The large termite's legs and pincers twitched spastically. She struggled to survive.

Irene detached the harness to her GlimmerLift and escaped into the tunnel. When she was about halfway through, the screeching stopped.

BRETHREN OF THE SAINTS AVAILABLE NOW

For young adults and up! The unique and thrilling adventures of Bud Hutchins, Maeve, and Ivy. They battle classic Hollywood monsters, avenge the dead, and save the world. Often. All the time actually.

Battle Monsters. Avenge the dead. Join the Order!

ALSO BY JB MICHAELS

The Tannenbaum Tailors series- An incredible world in miniature. Mutli-Award-winners. Bestellers.

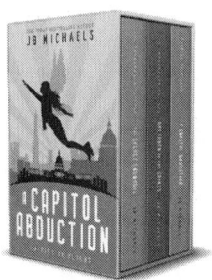

The Viking Throne! Experience the visceral thrills of "Taken" but on the high seas!